BROKEN BONES

BROKEN BONES

A NEW DAWN™ BOOK 6

AMY HOPKINS

MICHAEL ANDERLE

LMBPN

DISRUPTIVE IMAGINATION

DEDICATION

To all the parents who've ever had to work at home during the school holidays.
I salute you. You are warriors, and saints.

— Amy

To Family, Friends and
Those Who Love
to Read.
May We All Enjoy Grace
to Live The Life We Are
Called.

—Michael

CHAPTER ONE

Julianne looked down at the tattered ragdoll at her feet. It was splattered with mud and missing one of its little button eyes. She bent down and gently picked it up. She cradled it in her hand and wondered what had happened to its owner.

On second thought, maybe I don't want to know.

"What have you got there?" asked Marcus. He glanced at the small scrap in her hands and frowned. "I'm sure they got away, Jules. We haven't found any bodies so far."

"Course ye had ta bloody say that," Garrett grumbled. "Look."

The rearick jutted his chin at Polly as she stumbled out of a barn. Her face was pale and her eyes were rimmed with red.

"What do ye think she found?" Garrett asked quietly.

"Stay here." Marcus briefly gripped Julianne's shoulder and strode off toward the barn.

Julianne shuddered, but knew she couldn't leave him to deal with this alone. She took a moment to center herself, blew out a slow breath, and marched after him. She darted to the side as he and Garrett stumbled back out of the barn, Garrett almost stepping on her foot in his haste to evacuate.

Julianne gritted her teeth against the sound of Polly retching behind her. She prodded the squeaky wooden door open, then reeled back from the foul smell. She stumbled back, then sucked in a big breath of fresh air and plunged inside.

Her eyes quickly adjusted to the darkness, but she had a hard time dealing with the carnage inside. Rotting bodies covered the floor and blood and limbs were strewn about like unwanted rubbish.

"Well," Garrett said, peeking over her shoulder. "At least it weren't people. Well, not this time, anyway."

Julianne quickly realized he was right. Past the rotting and decaying dead flesh, she saw their clothes. Tattered and loose, some of them missing altogether, and all of them mismatched as if the owners had no idea how to dress appropriately.

There were broken teeth and crude handmade weapons scattered about. Still, she needed proof, and her eyes roamed the violent scene in search of it. There it was—a pair of red eyes staring lifelessly at the ceiling.

"*Remnant*," whispered Julianne. Relief made her limbs sag and she stepped back, closing the barn door behind her to stifle the cloying stench of death.

"Whatever they are," Polly said from behind her, "they smell even worse than what Garrett made for breakfast yesterday."

"Hey!" Garrett protested. "That were a fine meal."

"Yeah," Marcus interjected, "if you want to eat something that smells like *that*."

Julianne exhaled. "Would you three stop bickering already?" She held a finger up when Garrett tried to interrupt. "Not a word, you. You lot have been arguing since we left Tahn."

"They keep insultin' me cookin'," Garrett grumbled.

Julianne rolled her eyes. "Garrett, I know you miss Bette but it's making you crotchety. And I know you *think* you cook quite well." She steeled herself to deliver the blow. "But you don't."

She winced at the wounded expression on his face. "I know you try, and maybe..." Julianne grasped for something to say.

"Maybe it's just a regional thing? We mystics have our elixir, and rearick have the...the..." She gestured helplessly, looking to the others for support.

"The slop you made for breakfast," Marcus said.

Marcus, you're not helping, Julianne thought to him. Her eyes snapped the warning she couldn't say aloud.

He shrugged apologetically. "I'll stop complaining about your food, rearick. As long as you let me cook from now on."

Garrett snorted and stomped over to the remains of the tiny village. Julianne understood the prickle of unease that had the rearick on edge.

They had left Tahn knowing that danger lurked on the open road, but no one was willing to leave the outlying villages and settlements to fend for themselves against the monstrous beasts pouring through portals. At least, they *thought* there were more portals.

Ruefully, Julianne admitted that they were going by the word of a single remnant who had only divulged the information under threat of torture. But even if they had closed the only portal in the region which kept the strange Skrima from coming through it, there was still the remnant threat.

Why are they on the move? Why now, after all these years? The question tumbled about Julianne's mind endlessly.

The hordes were traveling the countryside as they fled from the threat—real or imagined—of the Skrima. They had descended on Tahn twice. The townspeople were prepared and fought the beasts, but there was a real concern that those in smaller settlements would not have the same capability.

Looking around, Julianne's heart was heavy. The remnant trapped inside this building were dead, and though they hadn't found any human corpses, whoever had lived here had still lost their town— their home. She just wished she knew where they had gone.

CHAPTER TWO

Twilight descended on the abandoned town and shadows stretched long over the grass. Glowing embers pocked the evening darkness, creating an eerie map of the buildings that had been burnt to the ground by the invading marauders.

"At least we have somewhere to sleep tonight," Marcus said. He gestured toward one of the intact buildings.

"Are you serious?" Polly screeched. "I wouldn't sleep in the house of a dead person if you paid me."

"We don't know that they're dead," Marcus protested. "We haven't found a single body to suggest they are."

"As much as I hate ta admit it," Garrett said, "the lad has a point. We'll be safer if we've got solid walls between us and whatever's out there."

"I'm with Polly." Danil shuddered. "Give me an open sky and plenty of room to run away any day."

"Of course ye'd run, ye pansy," Garrett retorted. "But I'm not freezin' me arse off just cuz yer a wee scaredy-boy."

"*Freeze?*" Danil scoffed. "You spent last night complaining it was so humid that your ball sweat kept dripping down your ass crack and making it itch."

Polly slapped him. "Thanks, Danil. I spent *all day* trying to get that image out of my head. Now it's stuck there forever."

"I can jump in there and take care of that for you if you want," Danil said with a wink.

"Not a chance." Polly slapped him again, this time hard enough to make him wince. "After what you did *last* time you were in there you're banned for life, Mister."

Julianne arched an eyebrow. "And what *exactly* was that?"

Danil coughed, Polly blushed, and both shuffled their feet. Neither answered her question.

"Look, whatever kinky mind-sex play you two are up to in your spare time, that's your business." Marcus winked at Danil. "Until later tonight, anyway—then I want all the details. But right now I feel like I've been dragged ass-backward through a meat grinder, so I'd really like to settle in and get some sleep for the night. Can we just decide where we're going to be sleeping, and be done with it?"

Julianne just watched as the fight erupted. Polly and Garrett argued and Danil backed Polly up, which only seemed to make the rearick more stubborn. Marcus occasionally threw in a point in Garrett's favor but seemed half-hearted about it.

"We'll sleep outside," Julianne decided, using a touch of magic to make sure they listened to her. "Danil, Polly, would you please set up camp on the outskirts of town? I'd like to have a look around before we settle in."

Julianne waited until the young couple had disappeared before gesturing to Marcus and Garrett. They followed her over to one of the smoldering buildings.

"What exactly do you think went down here?" she asked. "It doesn't make sense. How would you coax an entire group of remnant into one building?"

Marcus shrugged. "Maybe they set a trap of some kind. If the remnant thought there was an easy mark in there they'd be on it like flies on a turd."

"If the people 'ere were expectin' an attack they might have fled ta safety." Garrett scratched his whiskers as he thought. "Not a bad plan, really. Get the old an' the weak to safety, lure the bastards inside, an' trap 'em in there."

Julianne nodded. "Maybe these smaller settlements aren't as helpless as we thought they would be."

"When you're on your own you learn to survive." Marcus brushed her arm gently. "And I'm sure they *did* survive this. There's nothing to tell us otherwise."

Hot timbers cracked and popped in the cooling air and Julianne shivered. Indecision tugged at her . If they had abandoned Tahn to come on this wild goose-chase for no reason she would never forgive herself. Of course, if they saved just one life it would all be worth it.

Garrett let out an irritable grunt and stomped away. Marcus edged closer to Julianne and wrapped his arm around her shoulders.

"We're doing the right thing out here," he murmured in her ear. "*These* people may have gotten away, but we don't know who else is out there waiting for help."

"I know," Julianne said with a sigh. "I just hate not knowing what's going on."

They wandered toward the campsite. Polly had already erected the tents and Danil blew on a small pile of sticks that was just beginning to smoke.

"What's for dinner?" Julianne asked. She stole a glance at Garrett, willing to use a compulsion spell on him if he insisted on cooking again.

"I err... I have ta be..." Garrett's face turned beet-red and he scowled. "I'm busy, all right? Some other ugly bastard'll just have ta cook dinner." He stomped back into the town.

Danil laughed. "Thank the Bitch for that."

"I suppose I should slap you for that." Polly giggled. "But I'm as relieved as you are. Now, you two toddle off and do whatever it is you do while Danil and I make up for that awful breakfast."

"Just keep an eye out," Marcus told her. "We don't know what's lurking around out there."

Polly rolled her eyes. "We *know*, soldier boy. I swear you've reminded us of that every five minutes since we left."

Marcus gave a wolfish grin. "Then you'll expect me to remind you every five minutes for the rest of the trip too."

"I'm sure they'll be careful, Marcus," Julianne said. "Why don't we go find something to eat? If we don't replenish our stores we won't last the week."

"Wait a minute," Polly begged. "You're not going to look for food in *there*, are you?" She pointed toward the empty buildings.

Julianne shook her head. "No. There's a small chance the people who lived here will return. I don't want to take anything that belongs to them. They've lost enough."

"Try to catch something bigger than a rabbit this time." Danil ducked away from Marcus's glare.

"If you're going to complain about what we bring back, next time you can go hunting instead," Marcus growled at him.

"Let's go," Julianne said, "before you two find anything else to argue about."

Julianne unstrapped her staff from her horse and slung it over her back, then pulled a pair of shiny daggers out of her pack. Marcus raised an eyebrow.

"I haven't seen those before," he said.

Julianne shrugged. "Bette had them made for me. She said that as much as I enjoy beating things over the head with my stick, I at least need something sharp to cut my meat with."

Marcus snorted. "And I suppose it had nothing to do with the mess you make when you beat things over the head."

"You really think disemboweling with a sharp blade is going to be any neater?" she asked.

Marcus chuckled and walked into the dense forest

surrounding the little town. Despite the late hour, a full moon hung low in the night sky. Shafts of moonlight speared the canopy, allowing them to see.

"You *do* remember where you set the trap, don't you?" Julianne asked quietly.

Marcus shot her a dirty look. "Of course, I do. Mostly. I mean...I know the general direction."

Julianne was glad he couldn't see her roll her eyes. He and Garrett had set the trap before they'd reached the small town. They had hoped an offering of fresh meat would make the townsfolk more welcoming. When the two men had come back they were arguing loudly over the best way to prepare salmon. The discussion had nearly turned into a good-natured brawl. Polly had immediately laid a wager on them not being able to find the trap again.

Danil was the only one to take that bet, and this time he might have lost his money. It seemed that in the excitement of finding the town deserted and in ruins, Marcus really *had* forgotten where he'd laid the trap.

"I'm *sure* it was just around here," Marcus muttered. He squatted.

Behind him, Julianne slipped into a trance and embraced her magic, filling up to the world around her. In this state she had a tangible connection every leaf, every stick, and every grain of dirt. The sharp metallic scent of blood reached her nose and her eyes immediately cleared.

"Marcus," she said in a low voice. *You did leave your trap here,* she sent to him, *but something took your prize.*

Marcus froze, then silently stood up and drew his short sword.

Didn't you bring your rifle? Julianne sent.

Marcus grimaced. *It's back with the horses. I didn't think I'd need a rifle to catch a rabbit.*

I think we're about to catch more than a rabbit, Julianne sent.

CHAPTER THREE

Marcus and Julianne stood back to back in the stippled moonlight. They waited, still and silent as nearby leaves and branches quietly rustled in the darkness.

How many? Marcus asked.

He felt the subtle shrug of her shoulders against his own. *No idea,* she sent back. *Remnant minds are too fuzzy for me to get a real read from.*

I hope they at least put up a good fight, he mused a moment later.

You realize that's just asking for trouble? Julianne replied.

Damn straight. Do you know how long it's been since I faced a real challenge? He whipped his head around just long enough to shoot her a grin, his white teeth sparkling in the moonlight.

As if spurred on by his movement, the enemy attacked. Four scowling remnant, eyes glowing red above yellow crooked teeth, exploded from the trees.

"Told you I smell dinner," the tallest snarled to his friends.

Marcus groaned. "It was Garrett's cooking, wasn't it? What did I say? That stench is enough to attract every scavenger on Irth." He swung his sword and the remnant caught it in one hand, heedless of the blood that poured from its fingers.

"You need to stop giving him grief about that," Julianne said. "He's only trying to help." She lazily kicked a remnant back with one foot, then belted another in the knee with her staff. It crumpled to the ground with a scream.

Marcus slammed his head forward. Cartilage crunched, and the remnant howled. "That's the problem. He needs to *stop* trying."

Julianne jabbed the butt of her staff into the ribs of a remnant and her target coughed and gasped. A second thrust landed higher and Julianne groaned.

"Ugh. This bastard just got brain on my staff. Now I'm going to have to find somewhere to wash it." She shook the gobbets of flesh away, then ducked a flailing arm.

Marcus swung his sword and his opponent crumpled to the ground. Its head rolled away into the bushes.

"I'm just saying..." he continued, leaning one hand against a tree, "the only thing Garrett's cooking is doing is clearing the entire valley of anyone with a sense of smell."

Julianne smacked a remnant in the back with the head of her staff, then spun to clip the other in the jaw.

"Speaking of helping," she growled. "Are you just going to stand there all day?"

"You seem to have this in hand," he said, not moving. "I didn't want to cramp your style."

Julianne let out a grunt of frustration and Marcus was sure he heard her mutter something rude under her breath. He hoped it was just rude—he took heart from the fact her eyes didn't change color when she said it.

He didn't move, mesmerized by the graceful motions of her arms as she dropped her staff, drew the twin daggers, and leaned backward to avoid a spear thrust.

"Next time I'll leave you back at the campsite to cook dinner," she said. "Danil's getting better at fighting, but if he doesn't pull his weight against the beasts he'll at least wash my boots for me afterward."

"Sounds like Polly has him well-trained." Marcus snorted.

He was rewarded with a furious glare "Really?"

Marcus backpedaled. "I mean… He's trained to…to look after leather properly." He grinned nervously. "You know how boots get when you don't clean them right. Right?"

Julianne was silent, but he thought she was attacking with more force than necessary. She rammed her blade into the throat of one remnant and spun to kick the other in the midriff. As it stumbled back she continued her momentum and swept out a leg. She hooked her foot around the remnant's ankles and it tumbled to the ground. Julianne stood over it, panting for breath.

"I'll leave my boots outside the tent for you," she told Marcus with a glare. "And my robes. And my staff, too. And you *know* how much I hate it when my staff hasn't been properly scrubbed."

Julianne stomped away, ignoring the remnant who jumped back to its feet in a rage. By the time the beast had regained its bearings Marcus was the only one left in the clearing.

He sighed. "I deserved that," he told the remnant. "Really, I did. Unfortunately, you're going to suffer a lot more for it than I am."

A minute later Marcus strode back toward the campsite. A spray of fresh blood decorated his sleeve and he had a satisfied smile sat on his lips.

He ran his eyes over the four people sitting by the glow of the campfire. Julianne had already shed her robe and dumped it by one of the simple tents next to her boots and staff.

Julianne noticed his glance and raised an eyebrow as if daring him to sit down.

"I'd best get those clothes clean, hey?" He coughed awkwardly. "Before the blood gets dry and crusty."

"Sensible idea," Julianne said with a grin.

Marcus sighed dramatically and clomped over to the piled

mess. He bundled everything into his arms and disappeared in the direction of the ruined village.

"Should he be headed that way alone?" Danil asked.

Garrett snorted. "Aye. He's not a wailin' child—"

Something thwacked him in the back of the head and he scurried to his feet to see what had attacked him. When another slap stung his cheek, he spun back to Danil.

Danil shrugged and pointed at Julianne. Her white eyes were easy to see in the darkness.

Garrett opened his mouth angrily, only to have a sock stuffed in it. Not a clean sock, either. He coughed and gagged, trying to use his fingers to dislodge the cloth. As he swiped at his mouth, the eerie sensation of feeling an object with one part of his body but not the other made him dizzy.

He turned beseeching eyes to Julianne.

All right, I'll bloody behave meself, he thought, trying to form the words clearly in his mind.

The suffocating sensation vanished immediately. Garrett sucked in a breath, nostrils flaring in anger.

"I'm—"

All it took was a raised eyebrow from Julianne to deflate him. "I'm...thinkin' I might go help the lad wi' the cleanin'," he mumbled.

As Garrett stomped off, he swore he could still taste the lingering flavor of old sock in his mouth.

—

"Who's there?" Marcus called when he heard boots crunch on the dirt road. He gripped the wet staff in both hands.

"Steady on, lad," Garrett said. "I just came ta see if ye needed a hand."

Marcus narrowed his eyes. "*You* want to help me wash Julianne's stuff?"

The rearick nodded ruefully.

Marcus's eyes bulged, then a laugh bubbled up. "You did something to piss her off, didn't you?"

Garrett snarled and picked up a boot. He grabbed a piece of Julianne's robe that Marcus had soaking in a horse trough and started rubbing grime off the leather.

They worked in a companionable silence for a while, scrubbing and dunking, then changed the dirty water for a final rinse.

"I'm bein' an arsehole," Garrett finally sighed. "I'm just on edge, ye ken?"

"I know," Marcus said. "I mean, come on… demon monsters from the stars? Tiny villages at the mercy of hordes of remnant?"

Garrett dropped the boot he was holding and looked up in surprise. "What? No, lad. I'm just fidgety because it's been a whole week since me lady tended me nethers!"

"Your *what*?" Marcus choked.

"Me nethers!" Garrett grabbed his crotch for emphasis. "A well-endowed rearick like meself has considerable needs! Me balls are so heavy they're damn near draggin' on the ground!"

"That's because your legs end at your knees instead of your ankles," Marcus replied. "Your ass brushes the ground when you walk, too."

"Oh, that's low…" Garrett said. He flicked his hand in the water, sending a spray toward Marcus.

"Garrett! This is my last clean shirt." Marcus shook the water off with a scowl.

Garrett's face fell. "Ach, I'm sorry. Didn't mean ta be an arsehole about it. I only came over ta—"

He yelped as Marcus tackled him, his momentum propelling them both into the trough. Garrett gasped as the chill soaked through to his bones.

"Ye fuckin' bastard!" he wheezed.

Marcus rolled out of the trough and onto the ground, barely managing to hold himself up on all fours since he was laughing hysterically. Garrett struggled, unable to get purchase on the sides. A boot was jammed in his ass cheek and each time he tried to roll himself over, his only reward was a face full of water.

Eventually he stopped trying. "Get me the fuck out of here."

Marcus staggered to his feet and offered a hand. He helped Garrett out and steadied the rearick as he removed his boot and tipped a thin stream of water onto the ground.

"Sorry," Marcus said as Garrett shoved his foot back into it with a noisy squelch. "I couldn't resist. You looked so sad when you thought I was angry with you!"

"Aye, well. Been a bit of a crotchety old bastard, haven't I? I deserve a good thrashin'. Or a splashin'."

"What *has* got you so pissed?" Marcus asked, serious. "And don't lie—I know it's not *just* that you miss Bette."

Garrett shrugged. "It's like ye said. Beasts from the sky, and Bitch knows what's happenin' ta the people wi'out our protection. I feel like I shoulda been pushin' ta come out here earlier, but we had our hands full in Tahn with that bloody rift…"

"You feel guilty for leaving people to fend for themselves?" Marcus asked gently.

Garrett furrowed his brow, then nodded slowly. "Aye, I think I do. Bloody useless thing ta be dwellin' on, innit?"

"Useless is right," Marcus said. "We're here now—let's give those red bastards a run for their money while we are."

Garrett gave a resolute nod, then flung his head to the side and smacked himself in the head. "Water in me earhole," he explained, seeing Marcus's bewildered expression.

"If you thump the Skrima as hard as you just hit yourself in the head I won't need to lift a finger," Marcus pointed out.

"Can't get the water out unless I dislodge the rocks first!" Garrett chuckled.

CHAPTER FOUR

Polly carefully packed away the wooden bowls they had used for breakfast and drew the drawstring of her bag tight. Although Julianne had told her she wasn't responsible for menial duties like packing up the campsite and cleaning up after meals, Polly felt a sense of satisfaction in tidying up and leaving a campsite looking as though they'd never been there.

"Polly, do you have the map?" Julianne called.

Reaching deep into a saddlebag, Polly groped through the contents until her fingers brushed paper. She pulled it out and smoothed the creases before passing it to Julianne.

"This is the route we're taking?" Julianne asked dubiously, following one of the lines with a finger. "Why are we skipping that little village, Sweetwater?"

Polly leaned over the map to compare it to what Tansy had told her.

"That shadowed area along here?" Polly pointed to the section she was talking about. "It's marshland—really dense and boggy. Tansy said the troupe tried to pass it once and they almost lost two ponies. We'd have to backtrack along this road, then loop around. That'll lose us days of traveling."

"I see," Julianne said. "Once we've headed through Kells up to Anrock, we can come back this way?"

Polly nodded. "That's the route Tansy said would be fastest."

"I don't like leaving that nearby town vulnerable while we traipse the countryside," Marcus said from nearby. "Jules, are you sure this is the right choice?"

Julianne nodded. "We have to weigh the needs of the many against those of the few. Besides, what if we get there and it's been abandoned too?" She shrugged.

"We could split up," Danil suggested. "Polly and I could go to the closer location while you guys travel ahead."

Polly slapped him. "Are you stupid?"

"What?" Danil rubbed his arm.

"Haven't you *ever* read an adventure tale? When a party splits up everyone dies. Well, not the hero, but I'm *damn* sure that's not you." Polly crossed her arms and gave a decisive nod.

"I'm not the hero?" Danil pulled a face like a wounded puppy.

Polly's heart melted a little but she didn't give in. "You are to me, but let's face it…you're up against the mighty Julianne. If only one of us survives it'd better be her, right?" Polly flashed Julianne a quick grin and the Master Mystic stifled her own.

"I'm not the damn hero?" Danil muttered. "All this time I thought—"

"Polly's right," Marcus broke in. "We'll be safer if we stick together."

Polly breathed a sigh of relief. As bad as she felt about leaving a small town to struggle along without them for a while longer, she'd seen enough on their journey to know that the world had changed.

Remnant hordes moving en masse, the threat of alien monsters. Even the bandits had abandoned the roads, unwilling to take the risk against the threats that seemed to pour from every direction.

Julianne shrugged. "I'm with Polly. Besides, if what Tansy said about the locations is correct, it will take weeks for you two to catch up to us. We need you."

Danil turned a beseeching gaze on Garrett.

"Don't look at me, lad. I'm just the axe-swinger."

"Why are you so eager to split up anyway?" Polly asked, frowning. He hadn't mentioned wanting to leave the others earlier.

Danil pouted. "You have no idea what's in Sweetwater, do you?"

He was met with blank stares. It was the wounded expression on his face that gave Polly an inkling of what he was thinking.

"Danil, this Sweetwater place doesn't happen to make its own booze, does it?" she asked dryly.

A grin spread across his face. "Jakob wagered their mead was even better than elixir. We all know *that* can't be true, so I need to get some and try it."

A chorus of groans surrounded him. "You'd risk our lives— and the people waiting for us—for a drink?" Julianne asked.

Danil shrugged. "I wouldn't leave anyone hanging. I mean, if we went there first we'd still be saving people, right?"

Julianne's eyes flashed white. Polly didn't see the exchange between her and Danil, but he colored with shame and dropped his head. He kicked a clump of dirt with his toe, but when he looked up his expression was a little brighter.

"So it's settled?" Julianne asked.

Danil nodded happily.

"Let's move. We've wasted enough time in an empty village. Let's go find some someone who needs saving." Julianne walked toward the horses.

Polly ran to catch up with her. "What did you say to him?" she asked. "I haven't seen Danil change his mind that fast in…well, *ever*!"

Julianne snorted as she checked the straps on her saddle. "He didn't change his mind."

"What do you mean?" Polly checked her horse, then easily swung onto its back.

"Before we left Francis was running some calculations, trying to figure out where the other portals were. He thought if we knew which direction the remnant were coming from it'd give us a clue." Julianne mounted her horse and gave it a gentle pat on the neck.

"They're coming from Anrock, aren't they?" Polly asked quietly.

Julianne nodded. "In his eagerness to avoid riding straight into a portal he hadn't put two and two together. If the portal is near Anrock, its people are in the most danger."

Polly's heart sank, and not just at the prospect of Anrock being demolished by the time they got there. The only reason she hadn't spent the entire trip shaking in her boots was that she'd put all thoughts of another rift out of her head.

She thought about the silent conversation she'd watched. "What else did you say to him? Danil brightened up at the end."

Julianne grinned. "I bet him that I would punch a Skrim in the face before we got back to Tahn."

Polly's eyebrows skyrocketed. "He didn't bet *against* you, did he?"

Julianne nodded and Polly laughed. "You would think he'd lost enough money doing that. Never bet against the mighty Julianne!"

Lifted by the mystic's confidence, Polly kicked her horse and set off on the trail to Kells, determined that if Julianne really did punch a Skrim in the nose she would damn well do it too.

CHAPTER FIVE

"No, don't stir it like that!" Annie grabbed the spoon that was stirring a pot all by itself. "It has to scrape the bottom or it'll burn. Haven't you ever cooked before?"

Tamara raised a slender eyebrow. "No, I have not."

The Arcadian noblewoman really hadn't. At her manor there had been servants to do all that. Even since the revolution, during which her husband—idiot that he was—had sided with Adrien and lost everything, Tamara herself had been taken in by her family.

Oh, she could have helped manage the household. Bitch knew her mother, abandoned by her staff, could have done with the help. Tamara had rarely been home, though. She'd spent her days using every bit of magic she had to try and rebuild the mess that Adrien had caused.

"Scrape the bottom," she repeated. Tamara's eyes turned black and she waved her hand, this time applying just a touch of downward pressure on the spoon.

"Can't see why you don't just use your hands," Annie grumbled.

Tamara smiled. "If I'm going to teach physical magic to young students I need to keep my skills up to date. Besides, if my hands are free I can knit."

Annie eyed the pile of wool in Tamara's lap and grunted. "You'll be waiting a good while before that school is up and running. Won't happen while the world is all upside down like it is."

Tamara laughed. "That's *exactly* when schools are most needed. Keep the kids out of the way while the grown-ups do what they must to keep them safe. If my experience in Arcadia was anything to go by, giving children just a little bit of knowledge can be a powerful weapon in itself."

Annie peered into the pot of stew. "Looks like you've got the hang of it. *If* you can manage not to burn it, I'll go see to Angelica."

Tamara shuddered inside. After three weeks on the road with the insufferable woman, she'd rather scrub a latrine than pay her a visit.

"I saw that look." Annie scowled. "The woman is a simpering ninny, but she's useful. Try not to scare her away just yet?"

Tamara nodded, chagrined. "Of course, Annie."

The older woman stepped outside and closed the door behind her as Tamara wondered just how exactly Annie had come to wield so much authority over the two Arcadian noblewomen.

When they had arrived in Tahn and found the school initiative dissolved and the town preparing for battle, the Arcadian entourage had immediately made plans to return home. That had been weeks ago.

Instead of leaving, Tamara had been persuaded to stay at Annie's and help fortify the town, as well as provide food and shelter for the refugees pouring in from smaller settlements.

Angelica had been tasked with looking after the smaller children. She'd opened a crèche, teaching the young ones their letters and entertaining the babies. As irritating as the woman might be, she did have a knack for calming frightened babies.

Angelica's own children had adjusted less well. David and James had been raised as most Arcadian children were; well, the children of a rich and respected noble anyway. Spoiled and waited on hand and foot, the twin brothers had been shocked at the small rural village and even more flabbergasted when they had realized they would be expected to work for their keep.

Tamara shook her head, needles clacking angrily. Even Angelica, who doted on the boys and was responsible for their entitled attitudes, had been embarrassed at their loud tantrums and refusal to help.

Remembering the scene, she smothered her grin. *Bitch's oath! If Angelica ever finds out I was the one who switched their asses she'll string me up by the toenails.*

Tamara was pretty sure the entire town knew—after all, no one else in Tahn knew more than rudimentary physical magic. None of the townspeople had ratted her out though, and the boys were now mostly behaved.

"Oh, Charles," Tamara murmured, fingering the locket she wore around her neck.

It wasn't that she missed her husband. Far from it; in fact, she'd hated the bastard. His memory had spurred her to take control of her life after he'd died. After a lifetime of being told she was useless and pathetic, she wore his picture as a reminder to always prove him wrong.

She slipped the locket back under her dress. "If only you could see me now."

CHAPTER SIX

Marcus carefully stepped out onto the fat branch. It swayed a little under his weight, but was thick enough to hide him if one of the twenty or so remnant below happened to glance upward.

Hold back, Julianne sent. *Garrett isn't in position yet.*

What? Marcus scowled. *What the hell has he been doing?*

He needed something to eat. Julianne's thoughts came across dryly. *His damned stomach was growling so loud it was about to give us away.*

Tell him to hurry up, Marcus shot back. *I can't wait up here forever.*

Nearly ready. Julianne quickly touched Polly's mind as she watched Garrett sidle past two remnant basking in the dappled sunlight. *He must be almost on the other side, now*, Julianne thought. *Just a little more and we can...*

Garrett froze, and she jumped to his mind, knowing that despite his discomfort at mental visitors he would understand.

They had found the remnant band entirely by chance. They had been camped on a road near the path Julianne had elected to take. The group could have slipped by without being seen, but that would leave the remnant free to ravage the countryside.

The team had planned to surround the small horde and pick off the few on the edges, then deal with the rest.

Their plan depended on silently removing as many remnant as possible before they were discovered. They all knew they would need to work fast, so Garrett's sudden halt must mean something was wrong.

Julianne sank into his mind with a muttered phrase, taking in his view and feelings. His heart rate was elevated and his ears were straining for something. Sweat trickled down his back, running between—*ok, pulling back now*, Julianne thought with a grimace. She concentrated on his mind.

It was over there, Garrett thought, unaware he had a mental passenger. *Fuck me, maybe t'was me eyes playin' tricks...*

Then he saw it again—a flicker of red between the thick tree trunks.

Skrim, Julianne sent urgently to the others. She felt Garrett flinch as he too got the warning.

Before Julianne could sense what triggered it, he whirled to one side and hugged a tree. At the same time, the remnant camp exploded into action.

The Skrim launched into the swarm of remnant, darting to and fro with frightening speed. It stabbed one remnant in the throat with a long claw and it flung itself into the air to land on the back of another.

The Skrim was unfamiliar—standing knee-high, its front legs sported long needle-like claws that clacked as it ran but formed a strong dagger when clenched tightly. Back legs of insectoid appearance dwarfed the tiny body. They were strong and pliant, giving the animal frightening speed.

It's too fast, Julianne sent as it sprang again, stabbing a remnant eyeball three times before moving on.

The remnant ran to and fro as they tried to catch their wickedly fast attacker. It dodged and wove, dealing sharp slices as it avoided their clumsy weapons.

Still connected to Garrett's mind, Julianne felt his muscles bunch in anticipation.

Stop. This is not our fight. The Skrim doesn't know we are here. We watch and learn. Julianne felt a rush of disappointment flood Garrett's mind, followed by resignation. Once she was sure he would obey she slipped out.

The Skrim was fast and wielded a sharp enough weapon, but it was smaller than its foes. It left two remnant standing from misplaced stabs and faced enemy numbers that were probably greater than it could surmount on its own.

A club thrust upward as the Skrim jumped again. It clipped a leg and the beast tumbled to the ground.

The remnant screeched and howled, jostling each other as they tried to pile onto the fallen Skrim. It jumped again, this time clumsily, and almost missed its target. It buried one claw in a remnant's shoulder and quickly swung behind it as the remnant tried to grab the little beast.

The Skrim plunged a claw into the base of the remnant's skull and the thing collapsed, convulsing as the rest of the horde snarled and snapped, but kept their distance.

Julianne waited for the inevitable death...but it didn't come. The remnant fell still a moment, then its eyes snapped open.

Instead of the deep-red glow the damaged nanocytes bestowed, this remnant's eyes were a brighter and somehow more violent shade.

The remnant lurched to its feet awkwardly and twisted its head toward the horde.

As one, the horde screamed and descended on their fellow remnant. They ripped its limbs off as it struggled—not to escape or fend off the attacks, but to claw faces and sink chipped teeth into remnant flesh.

Julianne held her breath, waiting to see the outcome of the vicious battle. She blew it out slowly when the fighting ceased and the five remaining remnant pulled themselves away from the carnage.

"Find the bug," the tallest grunted. "Squash it. Make sure it is dead."

He stomped over to the still-smoldering fire and grabbed a black haunch of meat, tearing a chunk off with his teeth.

Three remnant rummaged amongst the bodies but one hung back, watching. It twisted its head to look at the chief and Julianne pressed her hand to her mouth to stifle a gasp.

The Skrim clung to the back of its neck, one claw firmly embedded in the base of the remnant's skull.

With a smirk the remnant bent and searched its fallen comrades, pulling back to reveal a knife. The blade was rusted and a little bent, but it was long and sturdy.

Biting her lip hard, Julianne closed her eyes for just a moment. *You can't warn them*, she reminded herself. *They'll kill you as soon as you speak.* It felt strange to feel the urge to save a beast from death mere minutes after she'd intended to kill it herself.

The Skrim-controlled remnant pounced, stabbing one remnant through the guts and whacking another in the ankle, taking off a chunk of skin and sending the beast to the ground screaming.

The chief turned around too late to save the last of his band, but strode over with his weapon raised high.

His opponent crouched low, then with impossible power it leapt furiously forward. The two remnant connected, grappling and clawing at each other, too closely engaged for weapons to be effective.

Julianne readied her staff. No matter how this turned out the survivor would not last long—not if she had anything to say about it.

The Skrim flashed into view as the remnant rolled, claw still firmly inserted into a now-bloodied skull.

Try to leave the remnant alive, Julianne sent.

Alive? Marcus thought back. *Are you sure about that?*

Julianne sent him the image of a human, eyes red, Skrim on its neck. *We need to know how they work*, she told him. *Just in case.*

She felt the punch to Marcus's gut at the idea of Skrima controlling humans but was reassured by the flood of conviction that followed it. She had no doubt she would get her remnant alive and kicking, the Skrim ready to be torn away and examined.

The chief grunted and rolled away, his bleeding chest wound giving some clues as to what had happened. The Skrim-controlled remnant clambered to its feet with a small bloodied blade in one hand.

Julianne readied herself to attack. Before she could move, though, a figure burst from the trees across the camp, screaming a war cry, axe blade glittering in the morning light.

"COME HERE, YE SCARY WEE SHITE!" Garrett screamed.

The remnant shot across the space between them. Its legs moved in an odd gait as it ran, since it was being controlled by something not used to human proportions. It scooped up a spear along the way, not breaking its stride.

Julianne snorted and stepped into the open. Marcus joined her a moment later.

"You think he can take it?" Marcus asked over the clamor of Garrett's continued yelling.

Julianne eyed the rearick, who had already taken off the remnant's hand. "No. If we don't help, that remnant doesn't stand a chance."

Marcus aimed his rifle and edged closer and Julianne ran forward with her staff raised. Polly and Danil dropped from the trees above to land behind Garrett.

The rearick twisted away from a clumsy stab and the Skrim screeched, the first sound they'd heard it make.

Julianne slowed as she approached, waiting for the perfect moment. Danil saw her and nodded.

"Garrett! Tower plunge!" Danil called tersely.

"Why the fuck would—oh!" Garrett caught sight of Julianne lining up a swing and turned his back on the beast.

Danil dropped to one knee and thrust out both arms, hands locked together. Polly aimed a listless stab at the remnant, more to distract it than to try to actually hurt it.

Garrett jumped, one foot landing on Danil's interlocked hands. The other foot touched Danil's shoulder as the mystic stood and thrust the rearick upward.

The joint forces of Danil's push and his own strong jump shot Garrett higher than would otherwise have been possible.

The remnant ogled the flying rearick. The Skrim, unable to anticipate the effect of the movement on the foreign life form, squirmed as the movement squashed it between the remnant's head and back.

When the remnant's head snapped forward, so did Julianne's staff. The Skrim caught the full force of the sharp blow and flew into the trees. Danil and Polly shot after it.

The remnant staggered and fell to one knee. It turned its head and snarled at her, eyes the dull deep-red of a regular remnant again.

"You're free?" she asked it.

The remnant spat. "Free to die."

Shrugging, Julianne nodded. "Sorry."

The remnant didn't move when she pulled a dagger from her belt, nor did it flinch when she stepped forward and placed the blade against its throat.

Despite the strange color of the remnant's eyes, it looked almost human. A grotty unwashed disease-ridden human, but human nonetheless. When she flicked the blade across the beast's throat, it crumpled to the ground and she spared it a moment of silence.

A crashing amongst the trees nearby alerted her to Garrett's return.

"Ye fucking wee roach, try ta run from me, will ye?" Garrett held the Skrim aloft, far enough away that the outstretched claws couldn't scratch him.

"I think it's been injured," Danil said. "But it still made us run after it."

"Give me a look," Julianne said. She stepped up to the creature, narrowly avoiding a swipe. The tiny beast hissed, whined, and screeched when she narrowed her eyes and called her magic.

Julianne muttered a spell and reached toward the tiny alien beast. A shield of static protected its mind, but she thought she might be able to press through if she tried hard enough. Even without breaking the shield stray thoughts and sensations slipped through, letting her see brief flashes of the Skrim's trip through the rift and its bewildering arrival on Irth.

Julianne couldn't see enough to guess where the rift might be —just a crumbled wall covered in plant growth, and damp with mold. It didn't look familiar, but Julianne wasn't surprised. If the portal had been anywhere people were likely to be, she was sure that rumors would have spread by now.

"Kill it," she said flatly.

Garrett grinned. "My pleasure." He grabbed the Skrim's head and gave it a quick twist, nodding in a satisfied manner at the crunch and dropping the lifeless body to the ground.

Danil kicked it. "What did it do to the remnant? It was like mind control, but he was doing it through these." Danil used the tip of his dagger to point at the long needle-like claws.

Julianne nodded. "We know they're connected to the nanocytes that give us magic; that's the same technology that created the remnant. And we know they have some form of mental magic. Well, I guess we can't really call it magic anymore."

CHAPTER SEVEN

Marcus was kicking through some of the debris on the ground and Garrett went over to see what he was doing.

"Lookin' ta see if they left ye a snack?" the rearick asked.

Marcus snorted and opened his mouth to make a comment about Garrett's cooking. Guessing what the soldier was about to discuss, Garrett waved his hands.

"Don't even say what yer thinkin'. I don't want ta get me arse handed ta me by Julianne. Again." Garrett knelt to pick something out of the rubbish at their feet. "Och, would ye look at that!"

"Is that a tiny screwdriver?" Marcus asked.

Garrett squealed in delight. "Aye, it is. Bette lost hers a few months ago and hasn't been able ta find one since."

"You'll be popular when you get home then," Marcus said. "If you're lucky, you might even get lucky."

Garrett let out a peal of laughter. "Lad, I don't need ta get lucky ta get lucky. I just have ta drop me pants."

Marcus winced. "Can we leave out the visuals?"

"Are you two finished picking through the remnant's trash?" Danil called as he wandered over to the two men. "Once Julianne has finished dissecting our dinner she wants to move on."

Garrett's eyes bulged. "Yer jokin', right? She's not really goin' ta feed us a Skrim fer dinner?"

Danil laughed. "Only if you keep causing trouble."

Garrett stuck his tongue out at the mystic. He was interrupted before he could come up with a witty response that wouldn't restart the age-old arguments about their unrefined pallets.

"Incoming!" Polly yelled. "Remnant horde headed this way!"

Garrett sighed and yanked his axe free from his belt. He hadn't even had a chance to clean it properly from the last fight. "Here we go again."

What Polly had neglected to mention was that the horde was already upon them, since the tiny campsite was swamped by screaming, howling beasts seconds later. They poured into the clearing and came to a halt, stumbling over each other when they saw the dead Skrim lying on a flat stone, separated at the joints and entirely dead.

One of the remnant at the front moaned. "They are cursed! The beasts have got the humans!"

The remnant horde snapped and snarled but didn't come any closer.

"What are they saying?" Garrett asked Marcus out of the corner of his mouth.

"I think they think we're being controlled by the Skrima." Marcus rubbed his mouth, trying to hide a smile of delight at the idea that remnant might be afraid of him. "They don't seem very eager to attack us, do they?"

Garrett shook his head sadly. "What a bunch o' pussies. Takes all the fun outta killin' them when you find out they're as scared as wee mice in a barn full o' cats."

Marcus looked at him skeptically. "I hope that doesn't mean you'll refuse to fight them."

Garrett snorted. "Not on yer life. As if I'd let ye take all the fun."

Marcus cocked his rifle. "Shall we go?"

In one fluid movement, the two men threw themselves into the confused and somewhat frightened rabble of remnant. It only took the enemy a few moments to realize that neither man had an alien passenger.

Garrett slammed his axe into the face of one remnant before he had the chance to raise the alarm, but even as he swung around and clobbered another over the head cries went out to rally their brothers to the fight.

"They just human scum!" the remnant screamed. "Wipe them out! Wipe them out and offer their bodies to the beasts."

Marcus withdrew his sword from a soft belly and spared a minute to turn to Garrett.

"Offer us to the beasts?" he asked. "Have they forgotten *they* are the beasts?"

He ducked and spun, slicing a nearby foot from the leg it had been attached to.

"Sell-out bastards," Garrett muttered as he sank his axe into a nearby skull. He squinted but didn't try to dodge the spray of blood that shot toward his face. "I can't believe the wee babies are so afraid of a few wee beasts that they would consider offerin' us up as tribute."

Marcus stopped for a moment to wipe the smear of blood from his face. "It's not like they've ever shown any loyalty. Even when they have a chief, they're just as likely to tear his head off as they are to follow him."

"That's different," Garrett said, taking a minute to catch his breath. He rested the head of his axe on the ground and used the handle to prop himself up. He heaved three deep breaths, then picked the weapon up again just in time to take off the arm of a remnant who slashed at him with a dagger. "Takin' someone's head off is not the same as layin' gifts at their feet and beggin' them not ta kill ye. I know which one *I* respect."

A quick look around showed that more than half the remnant now lay dead and Garrett and Marcus exchanged a glance.

"I'll take the left half," Marcus said. "You take the right."

Garrett gave a quick nod and grinned. He lunged away from Marcus into a group squabbling over who would kill the short bearded man.

When Marcus and Garrett split up Polly rolled her eyes. Oh, sure, either man would probably do fine on his own, but there was safety in numbers. She didn't understand this macho need to prove oneself by how many kills they could make in the shortest amount of time.

She balanced carefully on the branch and unwound the rope from her waist. She flicked it once, sending the tail end to loop around the branch, and a moment later it was knotted securely. She ran the length through her hands, eyeing the distance to the ground before tying it around her waist.

Polly ran a short way along the branch and dove off gracefully. The rope tightened around her waist and halted her body with a jerk well above the dirt.

She swung a bit as she dangled from the rope and slashed at the surprised faces of two remnant below her. As her forward movement diminished, she twisted to make sure that when she swung back the other way she would still be facing forward. She lunged to give her swing some extra momentum.

This time a remnant darted into her path and stood in front of her with both feet planted solidly on the ground. Polly grinned and waved as the remnant flew back, courtesy of the feet she planted in its chest.

"Best not get in the way of a girl on a mission," she called, swinging back for one last pass.

Another remnant tried the same trick but Polly didn't kick this one away. Instead she wrapped her legs around its head, flicked her knife to release the rope, and hurled her body backward. Her hands touched the ground and her abdomen clenched as the remnant's head smashed into the ground. Polly rolled to her feet and tossed away the last bit of rope that had clung to her body.

"I warned the last guy, but you lot never listen."

A hand touched her elbow and she flinched away, only just managing to hold onto the dagger she had been about to throw.

Danil stepped back with his hands in the air. "Sorry, didn't mean to startle you."

Polly grinned. "Who says you startled me?"

She flicked the dagger and Danil spun, only to find the remnant who had crept up behind him dead. Polly retrieved her dagger from its eye.

"Thanks," Danil said.

CHAPTER EIGHT

"Open the gates!" Bette called down. "We got incoming!"

"Good incoming or bad incoming?" Jarv called up.

"Yer openin' the gate, ye mushroom-brained idiot. Whaddaya think?" Bette shook her head and started to walk away, but paused when she realized Jarv was still standing there.

"Are we opening the gate and running out with our weapons drawn?" he asked dubiously. "Or opening the gate and acting like we're not about to kill whatever walks through?"

Bette groaned. "I told ye...if a remnant is spotted, we yell 'remnant,' not 'open the fuckin' gates so they can eat our faces off.' Clear?"

Jarv grinned and nodded, and Bette wondered if he hadn't known exactly what she had meant all along.

"You a'right, Captain?" Sharne asked.

Bette started to answer, but a yawn cracked her jaw and smothered her words. Instead she nodded, then wiped her watering eyes. "Fuck me, I haven't been this tired since..." She wracked her fuzzy mind but couldn't think. "Fuck it. I've never been this tired!"

Sharne nodded sympathetically, waiting for the creak of

moving gates to stop before she responded, "I feel you. The days have started to run into each other. I don't even know how long Julianne and the others have been gone."

Bette glanced at the watchtower wall. "A bit o'er a week. I don't think I've had more than a few hours o' shuteye in all that time."

The hum of anxious chatter floated up to them. "I'd best go down and see ta this lot. Yer a'right ta man the wall?" Bette gripped the doorway and lowered a foot onto the ladder.

Sharne watched and worried. The soldiers on rotation had been working hard, but at least their shifts ended every now and then. Bette hadn't left her duties at all, electing to sleep on a thin blanket on the watchtower floor for the few hours a day she wasn't on active duty.

"How about I take the new lot for their welcoming tour?" Sharne suggested. "You stay up here and have a nap."

"Thanks fer the offer, but I don't plan on comin' back when I'm done. I'm takin' me arse home, shovin' it inta a warm bed, and not comin' back till I've caught up on me sleep. Unless we're attacked." Bette shrugged. "In which case me plans will go ta hell in a handbasket."

"If you insist," Sharne said. *Of course*, she thought to herself, *if you don't know we're being attacked, it won't interrupt your beauty sleep, will it?* She resolved to make sure her leader got the sleep she needed, no matter what.

Bette clambered down the ladder, almost missed the bottom rung but managing to catch herself before she fell arse-first in the mud.

"Everybody in?" Jarv called from up ahead. "Closing the gates now!"

Bette regarded the sorry group of travelers. There were about fifteen in total, mostly old women huddled under thin shawls with small children clinging to their skirts or hiding behind their elders.

Bette crouched in front of a small girl who stood a little apart from the rest. She looked tired, and her eyes held the weight of what she had seen on the roads. Still, she stood tall and straight and looked Bette in the eye.

"Is this the safe place everyone has told us about?" the girl asked.

"It is, wee one." Bette offered her hand.

The girl didn't take it. "You talk funny," she said. "Does everyone here talk like you?"

"Abigail, hush." An older woman hurried over and tried to snatch the girl away. "I'm sorry for her rudeness. Please forgive her."

Bette sat back on her heels. "And what's rude about that? I *do* talk funny." She looked back at the girl. "There's another man here what talks like me, but he's out fightin' the monsters."

The girl's face brightened. "He's killing remnant? He must be very brave."

From behind them Jarv barked a laugh. "Garrett's brave, but he's not as brave as our captain. He's not as smart as her, either. He *is* a lot hairier, though."

A couple of the children giggled and Bette stood. "Come on, ye lot. Ye all look ta be in need of a good feed and a place ta rest yer heads. I'll show ye where ya can get both."

Bette led the ragged band of travelers to the Hall. The doors were propped open, and the cavernous space was already twice as full as when the theatre troupe had used it as their temporary dwelling.

Harlon sat at a table by the door, a stack of papers before him and a pencil in hand. "Refugees?"

Bette nodded and turned to those following her. "I'll ask ye all ta give this man here yer names. A lot o' people have been sepa-rated from family an' friends, so we're makin' lists ta keep track o' who's safe."

A woman stepped forward, younger than the others, with a

baby cradled in her arms. "You have a list of survivors?" she asked. "Please, is my husband's name on it?"

Others quickly stepped forward with inquiries about loved ones lost during their travels. Apparently the men from the village had gone first, hoping to find a safe place to lead their families, but they hadn't returned.

Those who had stayed behind and the women who were fit to fight had left next. Half had returned, telling terrible stories of red beasts and immense hordes of remnant.

Bette shouted them down. "Just give Harlon yer names fer now so we can move ye inside. The list o' survivors we've found is on the far wall over there. Ye can get meals down the end o' the hall, but I don't suppose I need ta direct ye ta that. Those o' us in the town have been smellin' that glorious meat all day." Bette's stomach growled when she inhaled.

Harlan pointed to a woman and lifted his pencil. "Your name and village?"

Bette wandered away, leaving Harlan to sort out the clerical duties. It had been his idea to assemble the list of incoming refugees. Some had already left, hoping Muir had more space and was better able to cope with the influx of people running from the chaos. She knew the larger city would take anyone who asked, but they were already bursting at the edges.

Bette sucked in a deep breath, savoring the scent of roasted meat, hot gravy, and fresh bread. She wandered toward the table of food to look for Annie.

"Oh. Hello, Angela," Bette said awkwardly.

"Angelica." The Arcadian woman's voice was brisk and Bette blushed. Still, the blonde woman smiled at her. "You look like you need a feed."

Bette shook her head. "This is for the refugees. I can get somethin' ta eat back a' the barracks."

Angelica clicked her tongue in a motherly fashion, which made Bette's hackles rise. "We sent food over to the barracks two hours ago. It'll be cold by now, though I'd be surprised if your hungry soldiers left any."

Without waiting for Bette to answer, Angelica piled the plate high with food and thrust it into the captain's hands. "You can't protect the city if you're falling down tired and hungry. Eat this, then go get some sleep."

Bette looked at the plate hungrily and clapped her mouth shut, just in case she drooled on it. "Thank you, but I really do need to speak to Annie, and probably Francis too. Do you know where they are?"

Angelica looked at her carefully and sighed. "I'm not going to convince you to sit and eat, am I? Very well, take that plate over to Francis' house. You should find them both there."

"Much obliged," Bette mumbled through a mouthful.

She continued to stuff the food in as she carefully picked her way past the press of bodies, bags, and blankets strewn across the floor of the Hall. By the time she made it to Francis's house, her plate was empty and she had licked it clean. With her free hand, she knocked loudly on the door.

Annie pulled it open, glanced at the plate, and shook her head. "Let me guess...you didn't even take a minute to sit down and let that digest?"

"It's digested a'right," Bette said, letting out an enormous belch. "Though if ye've got some more bread, I wouldna say no."

Annie sighed and took the plate from Bette. Although she was a stickler for good manners, she knew Bette had been working herself into the ground. Annie admired such ethics, and to be honest, would have gotten the young woman any damned thing she'd asked for.

"Was that a new lot of incomers I heard?" Annie called from the kitchen as she piled the plate high with bread, cold meat, and cheese.

"It was," Bette said. "It looks like the dregs of a village—the few that were left after their men went looking for somewhere safe to go."

Francis shook his head sadly. "We really need to get the word out. I can't stand the idea of these people wandering aimlessly and desperate to find somewhere safe."

"That's what Julianne is doing," Bette reminded him. She gaped at the plate Annie brought out and fell silent as she piled a roll high with meat and cheese.

"I'm just glad we had that circus group visit," Annie said. "We wouldn't have been able to feed this horde if they hadn't taught us how to do it."

Bette hadn't paid much attention to the logistics of feeding and housing large numbers of unexpected guests, but some of the Druids from Madam Seher's troop had set up productive gardens and shown them how to take care of a large number of people.

"They might have taught us how ta feed a bunch of people, but it didn't do shite for helpin' us deal wi' their losses," Bette said with a hint of bitterness in her voice. "The ones comin' in are mostly abandoned, or they've lost their loved ones. How do ye ease that kind of pain?"

"Not just the pain," Francis said quietly. "Their fear. These people…they remind me what Tahn was like while the Dawn was still around."

Bette frowned and took another bite of her roll. "Whrem thm…" She swallowed and tried again. "When the Dawn's spell was broken and Julianne freed yer people ye fought back."

Francis and Annie nodded. "We did. It gave us a purpose, and allowed us to heal a little," Annie said. "But these are monsters you're talking about. Remnant beasts, and creatures from another world. We can't send old women and babies out to fend them off with pitchforks."

The angry flash in her eyes made Bette wonder if Annie, lacking any other weapon, would have been able to fend off an entire remnant horde with a frying pan.

"Ye don't need ta stand on the ground ta fight," Bette pointed out. "I might just be able to come up with somethin'...if ye don't mind, Francis?"

Francis heaved a deep sigh of resignation. He knew that whatever Bette *said*, he really didn't have a veto in whatever she planned. He just hoped that whatever it was wouldn't leave him with too much of a mess to clean up.

CHAPTER NINE

Bette didn't have to wait long to put her plan into action. Francis nudged her awake just a few hours later with news of an impending remnant attack. Bette bolted off his spare bed and sped to the watchtower.

Minutes later she'd brushed off Sharne's plea to head back for more sleep and started putting her plan into action.

"Put that barrel o' spears there," she told Mack. "The other one can go at the other end o' the wall. Did Lewis bring the slingshots like I asked?"

Mack nodded, trying to hide his smile. So far none of the soldiers knew exactly what Bette was up to, just that it involved the refugees and a good old-fashioned dust-up with the remnant. "Who would have guessed that every kid in this village had a half-dozen slingshots to their name?"

Bette shrugged. "It's no sleepy farm village. Tahn is full of fighters—fighters these kids look up ta. Ye don't think they spend every minute practicing wi' the blunt sticks they call spears and trying ta hunt rabbits wi' those slingshots? When they're out there it's not rabbits they're huntin'. They pretend they're remnant and yell battle cries before they attack."

Mack frowned. "Yelling at a rabbit doesn't seem like the best way to get it to sit still. Don't the rabbits run off?"

Bette shrugged again. "I said the kids wanted ta be fighters. I never said they were *smart.*"

Mack chuckled. "I see your point. We really aren't the town we used to be, are we?"

"No, yer not. *We* are not. And right now that's exactly what these refugees need ta see." Bette stomped down the narrow walkway that topped the wall that protected Tahn. The incoming remnant horde was a small one—only about forty strong—which under normal circumstances wasn't really a challenge for her now-seasoned fighters.

For this fight, however, those soldiers had been told to hold back, make their kills slowly, and not wipe the bastard remnant out all in one hit. Bette smiled to herself. If she could pull off her plan, she had no doubt that the timid, quiet refugees would wake up tomorrow feeling brave and in control of their new situation, no matter how unpleasant it was.

"Incoming!" Sharne yelled. The afternoon light was just bright enough to pick up movement at the edge of the trees. Bette raced back along the walkway and through the watchtower and slid down the ladder, a boot and a hand on each railing.

She ran to the Hall and flung the door open, eliciting startled looks and a few squeals from the people inside.

"I want every single one o' ye ta follow me," she yelled. "I don't care if yer old. I don't care if yer young." She looked at a woman carrying an infant. "That one can probably stay," she added.

The wee child was struggling to find its thumb. Bette didn't know much about babies, but she didn't think it was big enough to hold a spear.

The refugees stared back at her dubiously and none of them made a move to follow her.

Bette scowled; She would drag them over there if she had to. "Come on, stop yer lollygagging. Ye've got work ta do, and I damn well expect ye ta do it." Eyes dropped to the floor in shame and one by one the refugees shuffled forward.

Compassion touched Bette's heart. Some of them were so old that she wasn't sure they'd be able to even climb the ladder. She should have thought this through better, but it was too damned late now.

Bette led them over to the watchtower and hustled them upstairs.

"Are you going to dangle us over the side like bait?" an old woman snapped.

"If ye give me cheek like that I will," Bette snapped right back.

"I don't know what you expect us to do up there," another woman said. "If you want us to fight, you might as well just send us out to die. None of us could stand up to those beasts."

"Yeah, we know there's a horde on its way. If we thought we could fight them, we'd have done that back in our village." The man that spoke had joints swollen with arthritis and was missing most of his teeth.

Bette just rolled her eyes. "Get yer arses up the ladder and ye'll see."

One by one the refugees climbed the ladder. Bette noticed a familiar face as a young girl climbed past her.

Big eyes turned to the rearick. "Are you really going to feed us to the remnant?" asked the girl Bette had spoken to earlier that day.

"Ha!" Bette said. "Ye ain't big enough ta make a snack fer one."

"Maybe, but I'd punch it in the face before it got a chance to eat me." Somberly, the girl turned her head away and continued to climb.

Bette smiled. She knew right in that instant that her plan would work well.

"Open the gates!" The cry went up and the gates creaked open just wide enough for Bette's team of fighters to slip through. Their numbers had swollen to a dozen on the ground, which left five on the wall to fight with projectiles. Today those five had been tasked with something else.

"I want every single person here who wasn't born in Tahn ta pick up a weapon," Bette called. "No need ta be timid. They're all for chuckin', so ye don't have ta face the bastards down there up close."

The refugees were still shuffling along the boardwalk and trying not to trip over each other.

"Are you sure you know what you're doing?" Mack asked her.

Bette nodded. "Help them all find a weapon that suits. I want every damn one of them ta take out a remnant before this night is through."

"That...might not be possible," Mack said. "There are more refugees than there are remnant out there."

Bette shrugged. "It'll have to do."

Mack supervised the refugees as each picked a weapon. Most of the older people chose spears or large rocks. As she had expected, the children were excited to take slingshots. Bette sought out the little girl who had spoken to her on the ladder.

"What's yer name?" Bette asked when she found her.

"Abigail," the girl replied. "It's a stupid name."

Bette laughed. "It's no' a stupid name at all." She looked at the long spear the girl awkwardly gripped. "Are ye sure that's the one ye want ta use? We've got wee slings here fer throwin' rocks if ye'd rather."

The girl shook her head and clutched her weapon tighter.

"Ok, then. Pass it here fer a moment," Bette said. She snapped the spear in half over her knee, ignoring the child's stricken expression. "Here."

Bette passed the shortened spear back to her, then lifted Abigail's arms to show her how to hold it correctly. "Ye can't be flappin' that big stick behind ye. It'll ruin yer throw. Now it's the right length, if ye hold it like this point it like so... Then, *vroom!*"

Bette mimed a throw and Abigail smiled.

"Do you think I'll kill one?" Abigail asked.

Bette shrugged. "Depends on yer aim. If ye practice though..." She turned her head and spied a barrel of spears nearby. Bette strode over and grabbed a handful and took them back over to Abigail. She snapped each to the correct length one at a time.

"Aim careful-like an' take yer time, but throw as many as ye can. I'm sure ye'll get at least one!"

Abigail jerked her head in a serious nod, then scowled at a passing soldier who eyed the stack of broken sticks beside her.

"These ones are mine," Bette heard her mutter quietly.

"Aye, that they are." Pride swelled in the rearick's chest, and she left knowing that her plan had helped at least one of the sorry band find some healing and purpose.

"Bette!" Sharne hissed from the watchtower. "That girl is what...seven years old? And you're teaching her to fight *remnant?*"

"Aye!" Bette grinned proudly. "She's got a good head on her wee shoulders. She'll do just fine!"

Sharne rolled her eyes but let the matter drop. "They're getting awfully close," she said, pointing at the horde racing toward them. "You're sure you want our guys to hold back?"

"Aye." She waited until Sharne had given the order, then leaned over the railing to call down to Mack, "Don't go killin' all those remnant! Leave some fer me helpers, aye?"

"Right!" Mack saluted. "*Don't* kill the ravaging monsters out for our blood. Got it, Captain."

"Get off wi' ye, smartarse."

Mack slipped through the gate and closed it behind him and Bette ran to the other side of the tower to watch.

Mack joined the soldiers, who stood in a neat formation. Bette swore she could hear some unhappy muttering drift up to her, but as the horde gained ground they dug their heels in, ready for the attack.

"Now!" Bette yelled the order along the wall. "Throw yer

weapons! Take the bastards down! And fer the Bitch's sake, don't hit me soldiers!"

A couple of spears flew limply through the air and fell well short of the remnant. One trailed the rest—thrown later, but with a strong arm and a good eye. This spear was shorter than the others…and though it didn't take a life it grazed a leg, making a remnant flinch and stumble.

"Aye! Ye got the bastard! Throw again, lass!"

Bette held her breath as another volley of spears sailed over the wall, this time flying farther and straighter. A couple stuck in the limbs and bellies of their enemies and a smatter of cheers resounded along the wall.

By now the remnant had reached the soldiers and they fought defensively, kicking the attackers back and leaving as much space between them and the enemy as they could.

A few stones whipped out, then a few more. Juvenile cries of delight joined the celebrating women.

"Ye don't have time fer a bloody party!" Bette yelled. "Get yer weapons ready! Throw! And again!"

Spears began to fly with regularity, the earlier success spurring them to try harder. A remnant screeched and reeled, clutching at the snapped-off spear jutting from its eye. He died quickly, but not before Bette pumped her fist in the air.

"That's me lass! I knew she'd get one!"

Sharne couldn't hide a smile, glad she'd been wrong about her captain's decision to bring the children in on the fight.

In a quiet moment a voice floated up from the ground. "Sorry!"

Bette leaned over to see what Mack was apologizing for and found him standing over two remnant bodies, his spear dripping with blood. He looked up and saw her disapproving glare.

Mack shrugged apologetically. "It was an accident! He tripped and…fell?"

"And the other one?"

"Oh, I stabbed *him*!" Mack grinned, then motioned at the wall. "Looks like you've got the beginnings of a new army up there, boss!"

Bette raised an eyebrow and gestured to a spot behind Mack. Without blinking, he twirled and kicked back the remnant who had come at him while he'd been talking. The remnant prepared to charge again, then dropped dead as a spear—this one whole—pierced its chest and pinned it to the ground.

"Aye," she replied thoughtfully. "I just might."

CHAPTER TEN

Julianne spread the crumpled map over her horse's flank, patting the beast as it flinched irritably. She squinted, following the lines with a finger.

"I think we're supposed to take the trail to the left, but this part isn't very clear."

Polly nudged her horse over and leaned down to take a look. "You know..." she began, then fell silent.

Julianne prodded her to continue.

"If we take the *other* path we'll know pretty quickly if it's the right way. It'll either curve left or keep going or turn in the other direction. If we take the one to the left it'll take a lot longer to figure out if we're on the wrong track."

"Good point," Julianne said. She refolded the map and handed it to Polly. "You're now the designated tour guide."

Polly yelped, "Me?" She shook her head frantically. "I just made a suggestion!"

"Yes, but it's about the fortieth good suggestion you've made since we left. I don't know why it's taken me so long to put you in charge." Julianne gave her a reassuring grin. "It's all right if you end up leading us the wrong way. Just blame it on Danil."

"Hey!" Danil pasted a wounded expression on his face. "Not fair."

"Well, you know what they say about life." Julianne climbed back onto her horse. "Come on, we don't have all day."

They followed the trail and Julianne's spirits lifted when it began to curve around toward the town they were headed for. Her hopes were dashed, however, when it soon dead-ended in a small clearing.

"Well, that wasn't what I—" Polly snapped her mouth shut when Garrett gestured for her to be silent and pointed at the bushes.

Through the mess of twigs and leaves, Julianne saw what had gotten him so excited. A beady black eye watched them warily and though the bulk of the animal was hidden behind the foliage, its antlers stood tall.

Julianne immediately knew that if they could snare this deer it would not only replenish their stores, but provide them with a hearty meal to offer the next town when they arrived. She stopped herself from adding, *if there's anyone left alive to eat it.*

Knowing that hunting game wasn't among her strengths, Julianne simply sat quietly. She stroked her horse's neck, praying it would stay calm and not scare the target away.

Behind her, Polly carefully reached back into one of her saddlebags. She lifted the flap and dug around inside, finally drawing out a small crossbow. Polly winced at the loud click the weapon emitted as she loaded the bolt, but the buck didn't move. She raised the weapon and rested the butt against her shoulder

The twang of a fired bolt finally scared the deer, but it was much too late. It flinched, then reared on its back legs, squealing. The sound was quickly cut off by a second bolt. The majestic beast was dead in seconds.

"That's dinner!" Danil exclaimed excitedly.

"Oh, Danil, how wonderful of you to volunteer to help carry it," Julianne told him with a cheeky grin.

Danil opened his mouth to protest, then cut off whatever he was going to say with a groan. "Every time I open my mouth... Every. Damn. Time."

Polly giggled. "We know you like to be helpful."

The team dismounted, and it wasn't long before the deer had been gutted, cleaned, and trussed at the ankles. Julianne winced as Marcus and Danil hung the animal from her staff, but admitted they really had no other choice.

Danil and Marcus—one end of the staff over their shoulders —led the way back down the trail toward the other fork in the road. Julianne rode beside Polly, with Garrett bringing up the rear.

"So much for my great navigational skills," Polly said ruefully.

"Those navigational skills netted enough food for a week, which ensures us a hearty welcome at the next town," Julianne pointed out.

Polly shrugged. "I guess so."

Julianne settled back on her horse, muttering a word as her eyes began to glow. She held her magic gently, using it to sweep her surroundings rather than send it out in any particular direction.

She felt no signs of human life nearby. There was also no sign of remnant, which should have been a relief, but the total silence was unnerving.

The road they now traveled was overgrown and filled with troughs and channels where the rain had cut rifts in the dirt. Anything this poorly maintained would not have been traveled frequently.

Of course, the closest village to Kells was Anrock, which was on the other side of it. It could simply be that in this time of unrest and upheaval, travel had been limited to the larger city.

"This is no fucking road," Garrett grumbled, echoing Julianne's own musing. "I bet me arse that no one has been along here in months."

"Are you trying to jinx us?" Danil asked. "Because I for one am hoping to find the town of Kells bustling with activity and doing a roaring trade in wine and prost—" Danil stopped speaking abruptly and snapped his mouth shut.

Polly dissolved into giggles. "Oh, Danil, I can't tell you how much I love it when you pretend to be a man of the world. You ride from town to town indulging in all the vices a man should—even though I know for a fact that before you met me you hadn't gotten laid in about three years."

Danil almost dropped his end of the deer. "Polly, you're not supposed to... How could you... Oh, Bitch curse me." Danil's shoulders sagged and he dragged his feet as he walked.

"It's okay, Danil. It's not like we didn't already know that." Marcus sniggered, then lurched back as Danil did in fact drop his end.

Danil raised his hands in exasperation. "That's it. I quit."

"You quit what?" Julianne asked. "Come on, it's not like you're not used to having everyone know your secrets. You spent most of your life in the mystics' temple, where *everybody* knows your business. Why start caring now?"

Danil shook his head in resignation. "It's not the same," he grumped. "I mean, just because a man has, you know...not been, it doesn't mean you have to talk about it in front of him."

"Then I guess it's lucky you've no longer 'you know...not been,'" Polly told him. "You've 'you know...been' recently; quite frequently, I might add. Oh, don't you go acting all offended. It's not like they can't hear you grunting and squealing."

Garrett gasped and doubled over, almost slipping off his horse sideways. He held his stomach, laughing so hard he almost choked.

"Come on," Julianne said. "Garrett doesn't need another excuse to slow down. We need to get to Kells by nightfall so I don't have to spend another night sleeping on the dirt."

"Sleeping on the dirt and listening to Danil grunt and squeal," Marcus added. He ducked Danil's right hook.

"Would you like to ride, dear?" Polly asked kindly. "I can carry the meat for a while if you'd like to take a break. Then we can save your stamina for tonight." She winked lasciviously.

The entire party erupted into laughter and Danil couldn't help cracking a smile himself. "I *do* have a lot of stamina," he agreed with a sly grin.

"Sometimes I wish ye had a little less," Garrett said. "Do ye know what it's like listening ta that all hours o' the morning when ye've left yer lady love back home? Who *knows* what she's doin' wi'out me. She might have run off wi' one of those wee soldier boys o' hers." Garrett's face crumbled as he contemplated the likelihood of his darling Bette falling for another man's advances.

Julianne rolled her eyes. "I think you're safe. I know that Bette likes her men with as much hair as a man can grow. I don't think anyone in Tahn can possibly match your prolific locks."

Garrett jerked up at that and grinned. "You're right. No one can grow a beard like a rearick can."

After some coaxing Danil finally allowed Polly to take his place. To soothe his damaged ego, Julianne insisted on doing the same for Marcus. The two women led the procession toward Kells while the three men rode behind them.

"What do you think we will find there?" Polly asked Julianne quietly.

Julianne shrugged, almost unbalancing the load on her shoulder. "I don't honestly know. I hope we find a town that is still thriving despite what's going on."

"And if we don't?" Polly asked.

Julianne heaved a deep sigh, loaded with wariness and the weight of responsibility. "Then we keep going. We traipse every damn foot of this countryside until we make sure there is not a single person hidden in some distant corner waiting for someone to rescue them."

Polly straightened a little bit at that. "That's a good plan. I like good plans."

CHAPTER ELEVEN

Marcus held an arm out for the others to hold back.

"There she is," he said.

The tiny town of Kells looked as empty as the last place they had visited. Its few ramshackle buildings had been tightly shuttered, and the single street that ran through it was empty.

"There are people in there," Julianne said. "Not many, but some." Her eyes glowed white and her face creased with worry. "They're afraid, Marcus. Their helplessness and despair... It's almost overwhelming."

Marcus nodded in understanding. He remembered the first time they had approached Tahn. The town had been under the influence of the new Dawn, and fear had soaked the air.

We saved Tahn. We can save these people too, he told himself.

"Be careful," he said aloud. "They might be afraid and feeling helpless, and that might make them unpredictable. We'll go in with empty hands, but be ready just in case."

He felt Julianne's mental nudge of reassurance. Marcus slid off his horse and gestured for Danil and Garrett to do the same, and they walked into Kells.

They wandered down the street, seeing no one, and hearing

no obvious signs of life though Julianne insisted there were people around. If not for her magic, he might have assumed the town had been abandoned like the last one they had visited.

"What do we do now?" he asked, unsure how to approach the citizens. They clearly didn't want to speak to the newcomers in their tiny town.

Polly shrugged. "We go knock on some doors," she suggested as if she was planning to go sell cookies in her neighborhood.

"Are you sure? I'm half-afraid someone will open the door and we'll find ourselves facing a sharp blade instead of a friendly face." Marcus shrugged his shoulders, trying to rid himself of the crawling sensation down his back.

He knew someone was watching him. Probably the whole town, in fact. He didn't blame them. If a bunch of strangers had wandered into his village he would want eyes on them too.

"This is ridiculous," he muttered. Marcus cocked an eyebrow at Julianne, guessing by the glow in her eyes that she already knew what he was planning.

"May as well try it," she said.

He cupped his hands to his mouth. "Hello, Kells!" Marcus bellowed. "We've come to offer assistance. We've brought food, and we have only good intentions. Please come out and speak to us."

Julianne grinned. "Well, that's one way to get their attention, and maybe a better one than pounding on a door. Knowing our luck, it would be a little old widow living on her own and terrified of the scary strangers."

"I don't think it worked though." Marcus looked around. Although nothing had changed, the feeling of it being locked up tightly had increased.

"Screw it," he said. "We're going to need to play this dirty."

He rummaged through his saddlebags for a moment, then stomped over to a spot roughly in the middle of the small village. Marcus dropped a tinderbox, flint, and a handful of the straw that he used for lighting fires into a small pile. "I'm off to get some firewood," he said and turned to walk away.

"What? Yer not going ta burn the place down, are ye?" Garrett asked, warily.

Marcus wheeled back, shocked. "No, you idiot. I'm going to cook dinner!"

"Oh!" Surprise and relief crossed Garrett's face. "You're going to *starve* them out!"

Marcus sighed. "In a manner of speaking. I'm hoping the tantalizing smell of roasting meat is enough to draw out at least one person. All it takes is one. Once they see that person fed, not hit over the head or attacked, others will follow." He cocked an eyebrow at the rearick. "Maybe you should come with me to get the wood."

Oblivious to Marcus's concern, Garrett grinned and nodded. "I understand. It's yer scrawny arms. Ye couldn't possibly carry enough firewood to cook this whole beast, could ye? No, no, no." Garrett waved his hands as Marcus tried to explain himself. "Ye don't need ta thank me. I don't mind pullin' me weight."

Julianne clapped a hand over her mouth to stifle her laughter. *Good luck with that,* she sent to Marcus. *Sometimes I really don't know how you deal with him.*

Marcus shrugged. *It's these scrawny arms of mine,* he sent back. *They stop me from knocking him out cold.*

"Danil, why don't you go with them," Julianne suggested.

The other mystic looked startled but nodded and the three men left.

"Do you think Polly and Julianne will be safe alone?" Danil asked once they were out of earshot of the village.

Marcus nodded. "The girls can take care of anything that might pop up, but more to the point, they don't look as threatening as we do. With a bit of luck, by the time we get back they will have already broken the ice with the people of Kells."

Despite Marcus's hope, he didn't allow them to dawdle for

long. They gathered the firewood as fast as they could and headed back into the small town. Disappointingly, Polly and Julianne still stood exactly where they had left them, alone and with frustration evident on their faces.

It was a good idea, Julianne sent Marcus. *But these people are just too afraid.*

But are they hungry? he sent back.

Julianne smiled hopefully. *Starving. Though come to think of it, so am I.* Aloud she added, "Let's get this fire going so we can eat."

Marcus squatted to light the fire and listened to Garrett talking to Julianne behind him.

"Why can't ye just use yer magic make them not afraid anymore?" he asked the mystic.

Julianne sighed "I could, but it's a bit unethical. Changing a person's emotions like that changes the choices they make. It takes away their freedom to act however they normally would. Plus, we can't predict how they'll react when we leave. When you force the fear out of a person, it often comes back stronger when the spell wears off."

Garrett nodded in understanding. "Woulda been a wee bit easier than all this standin' around though, aye?"

By the time Marcus had served up five bowls of hearty venison and vegetable stew, he was almost ready to give up hope. Despite the tantalizing aroma that drifted from their pot, not a single door had opened and not a single curtain had been drawn back. Marcus sat down next to Julianne with a thump.

"I really thought this would work," he muttered.

"Don't be so sure it didn't," Julianne murmured quietly. "Look over there."

Late afternoon shadows obscured the doorway that Julianne had pointed out, but Marcus watched as a strip of black widened and a pale face appeared. The face was followed by a body as a frail old man slipped out the door and closed it firmly behind him. He sidled over to the group clutching a small bowl in his hands.

Marcus casually moved over to make a spot at the fire for their guest.

The man fidgeting nervously behind him. "I know why you did this," he said in a weak voice. "Trying to lure us out with the smell of food, thinking we've spent the last weeks starving. Well, it worked. No one in this town has had a solid meal for over a month. You can kill me if you like, but if you do it before you share a bowl of stew I'll come back and haunt you until the end of your days."

With a quick nervous movement, the man sat down beside Marcus and proffered his bowl.

"No one is going to hurt you," Marcus said gently. "Or anyone else in Kells."

He waited for Julianne to speak, but she nodded for him to continue. "We've come from Tahn. Lord Francis—given the title by Lord George of Muir—sent us out to see if any of the outlying villages and towns need assistance."

The man snorted but licked his lips as Garrett filled his bowl. After the rearick had passed it back the man popped a piece of meat into his mouth, ignoring the scalding heat as he chewed and quickly swallowed.

"This is a small town," he said, stopping to eat another morsel. "I don't know any of those places you're talking about, and I don't know any of those people. I know about the remnant, though. No one would venture out and risk an attack from them unless they thought they could profit from it. And when one man profits, it's usually off the back of another." He stopped talking to shovel more food into his mouth now that the meal had lost some of its heat.

"I don't know what kind of people you've met out here," Marcus said, "but we hail from a long way away. We come from a place where people do their best to look after each other. When we came to Tahn last year, we found the people there had similar values. We helped them, and we'll help you."

The old man didn't speak. He chewed his mouthful of food, swallowed noisily, and tipped the bowl up to gulp the last of the gravy.

"What's your name?" Julianne asked.

"Jackson," the old man answered softly. He was silent for a few minutes as he mulled over their words. "You really just came to help?"

Marcus nodded. "It's what we do. In the morning, gather your people. We'll bring you with us—all of you—and take you somewhere safe."

Jackson sighed and shook his head. "As much as it pains me, I have to decline your offer. This town…these people. All we have left is each other and this place. We know our days are numbered, and we've come to terms with that."

"You can't stay here," Marcus insisted. "Even Anrock must be safer than here. Or come with us to Tahn. We have the defenses to keep out the remnant and the Skrima and there's enough room—"

Jackson stood, abruptly cutting off Marcus's words. He cradled the empty bowl in his hands. "If you mean what you said about helping you'll leave some of the food. You can sleep in the building over there. It's a bit drafty since it's been abandoned for some months now, but at least it's a roof over your heads. We'll expect you to be gone in the morning."

Without a word Jackson turned his back on the fire and the rich food and walked back to his house. The door opened a moment before he got there, leaving Marcus to wonder who was inside. Whoever it was, Jackson had just doomed them to a terrible fate.

"Don't be so morose," Julianne scolded quietly. "For all we know these people will be fine. They've lasted this long, after all."

Marcus gaped at her. "How can you be okay with leaving? These people are defenseless and starving!"

Julianne frowned. "I'm far from okay with it, Marcus, but if that's their choice—"

"*Choice?*" Marcus asked. "You've got the word of one man. *One.* Who's to say he speaks for everyone here? How do we know that's what these people *want*?"

He scowled at Julianne, but she gazed back at him steadily. It took a moment for her meaning to sink in and when it did, Marcus's heart sank.

"He really *does* speak for all of them?" he asked weakly.

Julianne nodded. "It's a tightly-knit town. They've gotten very close, especially since they've been cut off from everyone else. They trust Jackson to lead them. From what I've seen in their minds these people would follow him anywhere, as terrified as they are."

Marcus snorted. "I seem to remember there being a few people who would follow Rogan anywhere too."

Julianne clicked her tongue. "You don't think I'd know if something like that was going on?"

Marcus tossed his bowl to the ground, fighting to squash the irritation that rose inside of him. "It's just not right!" he cried. "We can help them. We can take them somewhere safe! Why wouldn't they want that?"

Julianne rested a hand on his shoulder and Marcus felt a wave of compassion and understanding flood in. He more than anyone knew that Julianne understood his point. It must frustrate her just as much, but she had the added burden of *feeling* these people's minds.

"I'm sorry, Jules." Marcus leaned into her and she wrapped her arm around his shoulder. "I just wish it was different."

"Me too."

Julianne and her team did as Jackson asked. Marcus washed the bowls at a nearby water pump and left them stacked neatly by the fire, where the large pot of venison stew bubbled. They gathered their belongings and closed themselves into the little hut that Jackson had directed them to. It was small and cramped and smelled like old dust.

As soon as the door had closed behind them Marcus ached to open it again. To compensate, he cracked the windows and took in a deep breath of fresh air.

"Stay away from the windows," Danil said quietly. "They're starting to look outside, to see if it's safe to go for the food. I think that if they see us watching it will scare them off."

"I can't imagine what it would be like to live in such fear," Polly murmured with a hint of sadness in her voice. "I don't know how you could call it living."

Marcus clenched his jaw to hold back his agreement. This town, these people… They didn't make sense to him. Raised as a warrior, there was nothing inside him that could relate to the defeatist attitude these people held.

"Remember, you had the love and support of your family, the training of a soldier, and thick walls and sharp weapons between you and danger when it threatened," Julianne reminded him. "These people have only known loss. There is *nothing* between them and the monsters outside. They know that any moment can be their last, and they accepted that a long time ago."

Marcus didn't answer. He just lay down his bedroll, turned his back, and tried to go to sleep.

CHAPTER TWELVE

Marcus didn't think he'd be able to sleep, but when dawn sent the first cracks of light seeping through the window he shook off the last vestige of sleep with surprise.

He felt stiff and sore and had the gritty eyes of someone who'd had a restless night, but he sat up. He took a moment to watch the motes of dust swirling in the sunbeams that pierced the gaps in the timber cladding the little hut.

Garrett's snores almost shook the beams that held up the roof, but Julianne and Danil both seemed to be sleeping through it just fine. Across the room, Polly stared back at him with sad eyes.

"I know there's nothing we can do," she whispered, "but that doesn't stop it from hurting."

Marcus nodded, trying to ignore the pain of understanding. He would sacrifice *anything* to change these people's minds; to force them to accept the help that had been offered. He would give one of his limbs just to see their faces light up with hope and experience the joy of truly living.

Marcus stood and rolled his head to work the knots out of his shoulders. His movement roused the others, and it didn't take long before they were up and packed to go.

"They didn't even steal a horse!" Garrett exclaimed when he cracked the front door and peered out. "They were tied there all night and they're all still there!"

Julianne snorted. "Not everyone thinks like a rearick."

"What's that supposed ta mean?" Garrett asked in mock offense.

"So, we're just going?" Danil asked.

Julianne nodded. "If we see Jackson this morning I'll try to change his mind again. Nothing forceful, mind you."

Danil heaved a sigh. "These damn ethics of yours are going to get this whole town killed," he muttered, but before Julianne could protest he waved her down. "Oh, I know, I know. If we took away their free will, that would make us as bad as Rogan. Still, there must be *something* we can do."

"Not unless they want us to," Julianne told him firmly.

She nodded to Marcus and he reluctantly began to gather their things. He piled blankets and clothes into bags and strapped his rifle to his back. In a few minutes he was done.

"Well, I guess that's it," he said quietly.

Marcus stepped outside before the others, shading his eyes against the sudden glare. Once he'd adjusted to the bright morning light he saw Jackson waiting patiently.

Marcus waved to him and the old man hobbled over.

"Didn't seem right to let you go without a thank you," Jackson said.

"Or to trust we'd go without a fight?" Marcus asked, noting the slim sword strapped at Jackson's waist.

Jackson spread his hands apologetically. "I told you...I have to take care of my people."

Filled with a sense of urgency on behalf of the people they were leaving behind, Marcus's brain scrambled for something to say that might change the old man's mind. "We could stay, Jackson. We could teach you how to fight them off."

Jackson gave a sad laugh. "That would just be drawing out the inevitable. Go, friend. Go and save the people who *want* to be saved and forget about us. There's no need to feel bad about it. We won't be around to care for much longer."

Marcus's heart twisted, but he saw there would be no arguing with the man. His eyes raked the little village one last time, desperately hoping to see a curtain twitch or a door creak open to reveal the pleading face of someone who would accept their help.

Nothing moved. It seemed everyone in this little town was resigned to their deaths.

"We've left what food we could," Julianne said. "Goodbye, Jackson."

Jackson raised one hand and waved with his fingertips. Marcus bit down hard on his frustration and pulled himself onto his horse, then rode out of town without looking back.

"This is bullshit," Polly said after a few minutes of silence. "I'm going back. I don't care if they won't come with us. I'll stay with them. Even if I have to fight off a whole damned horde of remnant all on my own." She wheeled her horse around and took off.

Danil turned pleading eyes toward the Master Mystic.

Julianne rolled her eyes and nodded. "Go on, you lovesick fool. See what you can do. Try to change their minds before we pick you up on our way home."

Danil saluted. "Thanks, Jules!"

"What the fuck are they doin'?" Garrett screeched. "How are the three of us goin' ta tackle a big ragin' horde if we come across one? Bitch's sake, how are *they* goin' ta fight off a whole horde if it attacks Kells?"

Marcus laughed. "Garrett, I've seen you fight. You could take on the biggest remnant horde we've ever seen all by yourself if you wanted to. I'm convinced the only reason anyone else gets a kill in is because you feel sorry for us and don't want to bruise our fragile egos."

Garrett smiled coyly. "Aye, yer right." He scowled again. "But they're signin' their own death warrants fer people what don't even want 'em there!"

"The people of Kells chose not to come with us, and I had to accept that choice—just like I have to accept Danil and Polly's choice to go back." She shrugged. "If they get into any trouble, I'm sure Danil will let us know." She raised her hand and waggled her wrist, letting the communication bracelet sparkle in the sunlight.

Garrett brightened. "So if they see a horde we can go back and fight it too?"

Marcus barked a laugh. "I knew it wasn't like you to worry so much about Danil's safety. You just don't want to miss out on a fight!"

Garrett grinned and nodded. "That weaselly little mystic is only nine kills behind me this trip. Can ye imagine what the bastard's ego will be like if he gets to kill twenty remnant and I miss out?"

Julianne kicked her horse to make it go a little bit faster, shaking her head. "Men!"

At least when Polly had been with them there was someone who understood the trials of traveling with boys. Now that she was gone, Julianne didn't even have anyone to complain to. She debated using Margit to bear the brunt of her rants since she wasn't limited by mere geography, but knew the old woman's sly wisecracks wouldn't help the situation at all. Besides, she probably had her hands full since she was doing Julianne's old job at the temple..

"Let's get this trip over with," she said. "The sooner we figure out the situation in Anrock, the sooner we can head back to pick up Danil and Polly...and hopefully the rest of Kells." With a pointed look at Garrett she added, "And any remnant we run into, we fight together."

They rode on, and Julianne tried to tune out Garrett's and

Marcus's discussion as they argued over how many kills Danil really had.

The point of contention was whether a remnant who had tripped and fallen onto a spear that Danil had shoved through one of its kin counted.

Marcus was quite adamant that it did, because Danil had been holding the spear at the time. Garrett argued that intent mattered more than action. Danil hadn't intended for the second one to die right at that precise point in time, so the death didn't count toward Danil's total.

Skrima! Danil's voice echoed through Julianne's head as loudly as if he'd shouted it right next to her.

Julianne wheeled her horse around and kicked it hard. She didn't bother to call to either of her companions, trusting them to follow without question. As she raced back to the tiny village they had left not an hour before, she hoped they would not be too late.

CHAPTER THIRTEEN

"Go, go, go!" Polly ushered the women and children past her, almost shoving them through the tiny door to the underground cellar.

"Hurry up!" Danil yelled, his voice distant because he was at the other end of the tiny town.

"Is that everyone?" she cried.

"Shut the door!" Jackson yelled, still standing outside.

Polly spared him a glance. He gave a small shake of his head. "I'll fight—or I'll try, anyway. It might not make a difference, but I'll try."

A woman pushed her way out before Polly could slam the door shut. "So will I!" she said firmly.

Polly sighed impatiently. "Anyone else willing to join the army of four?"

After the slightest hesitation, three more people barreled out. A moment later, the door was locked.

Polly turned to her unexpected team of fighters.

"You." She pointed to a man who, though clearly younger than Jackson, was still old enough to be her grandfather. "What's your name?"

"Travis, Miss." He licked his lips nervously.

"Ok, Travis. Stay here and watch this door. If *anyone* comes near it, scream for help. Don't try to fight them until you've done that. If you die and we don't know the bad guys are here, everyone in that room is screwed."

The man turned a sickly shade of green but nodded. He planted his feet and clenched his fists. "You can count on me."

She turned to the others. A middle-aged woman, Jackson—who was as old as the hills, and two more men were all she had. None of them looked like fighters. In fact, none of them looked like they could survive an altercation with a four-year-old street kid.

"If you want to survive—if you want your people to survive—this is not the time for heroics." Polly glared at them, waiting for her words to sink in. "Run like hell, distract them if you can, and stay out of our way. If you can buy Danil and me some time we *might* just win this thing. We can't do that if we're trying to save your arses."

Leaving them with those basic instructions, Polly took off running. Her feet flew over the bumpy unkempt street that ran through the town, ears straining. She couldn't see Danil, and she couldn't hear him anymore either.

She passed a small building, and the door exploded. Two remnant burst out, eyes glittering an unearthly red. One smiled slowly, and the other leapt toward her faster than any remnant should be able to move.

Polly used her momentum to throw herself into a roll, barely avoiding the remnant's grasp. By the time she was on her feet, she held a long dagger in each hand. One of the remnant slid to a stop and crouched before her.

"Die," it said, and jumped toward her.

Polly flung herself to the side as she saw the small rock that shot toward the remnant's head. It wasn't enough to hurt the beast, but it caught its attention. The remnant, thrown off balance by the rock, stumbled as it landed. That was all Polly needed.

She slipped around it and planted one of her daggers in its calf. She didn't stop to examine the damage, only prayed it would slow the creature enough for her to dislodge the tiny red beast that clung to the back of its neck.

A whisper passed behind her and she ducked reflexively. Her instincts were good…the second remnant had come up behind her and she narrowly avoided its dive.

Instead of gripping the girl's slim waist, the remnant stumbled over her crouched form and tumbled to the ground. Polly slammed her body onto her target as she raised her blade.

Burning pain flared in her ankle and Polly screeched in pain and terror, trying to dislodge the teeth of the remnant who had attacked her. Her booted heel caught it in the eye and it pulled back, tearing the flesh and tendon still clenched in its teeth.

Polly screamed again but didn't stop fighting. She kicked wildly with her uninjured foot even as she struggled to hold down the beast beneath her. She heaved a sob of relief as a large rock smashed into the head of the remnant at her feet.

A trembling Jackson stood over it, face as white as the sheets on her bed at home. He panted, chest heaving at the exertion of lifting the large stone.

One remnant was dead, but the other still struggled beneath her. Polly pinned its arms with her body and slipped a knife into the small space between the Skrim and the remnant's skull. With a flick of the blade, she dislodged the alien beast.

The Skrim let out a piercing shrill whine and the remnant fell silent. Polly slashed her knife again and split the Skrim in two. Polly groaned in relief when the sound ceased.

She rolled off the remnant but flinched as it scrambled away from her. The remnant raised its hands to the back of its head, scrabbling and clawing at the wound the Skrim had left. It yanked hard, drawing out a long thin tentacle that still writhed in its hand. The remnant bashed the squirming appendage against the ground, smashing it over and over again until the thing fell still.

Eyes now faded to the normal dark-red of a remnant, the beast turned frantic eyes toward Polly. She pulled herself backward, one leg useless and trailing blood behind it as she inched away. The remnant bared crooked yellow teeth, then ran off into the forest.

"The fuck?" Polly whimpered. She looked up at a clatter nearby. "Danil!"

Jackson shook his head. "You're going nowhere."

Polly narrowed her eyes. "Wanna bet?"

She raised a hand and gestured at him. When he tipped his head, bewildered, Polly said, "Your shirt."

"My...shirt?"

"Well, I'm not taking off mine!"

She waited impatiently for Jackson to pull the garment off and hand it to her. Gritting her teeth against the pain, she tore off a wide strip. She grimaced at the dirt caked around her wound and wondered what the hell kind of bacteria had been in the remnant's mouth, but she nonetheless bound her ankle tightly. With Jackson's help, she pulled herself to her feet.

"Daggers." She pointed at the weapons on the ground and Jackson scurried over and picked them up.

A thought struck him. "Stay here," he directed as he hurried off.

Well, I think *he's trying to hurry,* Polly mused as she watched the arthritic old man hobble over to one of the buildings.

It took a moment to recognize it as the little house he had emerged from the previous night. In the light of day, the faded and peeling paint that suggested it had once been a bright and happy little building.

Jackson disappeared inside, but the door hadn't finished swinging shut before he emerged again. He hurried back to her, this time moving faster as he leaned on a finely carved cane. When he reached her, he handed it to her.

"This might help," he offered. Polly took it gratefully but his hand lingered on the stick. "I... Thank you. I was wrong. I shouldn't have sent you away."

"You're damn right about that," Polly agreed. She flashed him a grin. "Lucky for you we're stubborn bastards."

Polly gingerly took a step, wincing as her injured ankle took her weight. She used the cane to take some of the pressure off the foot and looked down at the pair of daggers clutched awkwardly in one hand. *This won't do.*

She turned back to Jackson and passed him one of the knives. "Use this, or, find someone who can. I want it back when the fight's over, so don't lose it."

Jackson's eyes widened as he took her weapon and he nodded once, looking for all world as if she had just handed him a crown dripping with jewels.

Hearing another crash—this time just on the other side of the building she was next to—Polly waved him away. "Thanks for the help, now go!" She banished the old man from her mind and painfully made her way around the building.

She found Danil wrestling a remnant with no weapon in sight. The beast gnashed its teeth a bare finger's width away from his neck. Danil jerked a knee up, planting it into the remnant's groin, but the beast didn't even flinch.

"I knew you cowards had no balls," Polly jibed.

She dropped the cane and straightened carefully, putting her weight on her good leg, and threw her dagger. As the blade flicked end over end through the air, Danil leaned one shoulder back and turned the remnant around to meet the approaching weapon.

The blade struck hilt-first, clattering against the Skrim's hard shell. Though it hadn't been the strike she'd intended, Polly sucked in a joyful gasp when the impact knocked the Skrim free.

The remnant staggered back and the Skrim darted to one side, beady eye stalks turning in two different directions as it took stock of its surroundings. Danil slowly crouched and slipped a knife from his boot, but as he drew it out the Skrim shot toward him.

The remnant bolted forward, anticipating the alien creature's attack. It snatched the tiny beast mid-flight and slammed it into the dirt. The hard shell cracked and intestines splattered, coating the remnant's hands. It continued to pound even after the creature was clearly dead.

The remnant screamed, punching the small red beast repeatedly until the skin tore from his knuckles and his hand was mangled and broken.

Finally the remnant stood and spat on the ground next to the massacred beast, then glanced toward Polly and Danil.

Danil braced himself for an attack, but Polly just watched. Dull red eyes met hers and she nodded once. The remnant slowly walked away.

"Where is he going?" Danil asked.

"Let him go," Polly told him slowly. "There's something weird going on here, Danil."

"'Weird' is right," he said. "I've *never* seen a remnant walk away from a fight."

Polly retrieved her dagger from the ground and her hobbling movements caught Danil's attention. He rushed to her side. "Are you hurt?"

"One of those Skrim-fucked pricks tried to chew my leg off," she informed him as she brushed away his attempts to help her walk. "Don't you dare start smothering me! Not in the middle of a fight, anyway. We have more aliens to kill."

Danil stood back with a grin. "Yes, ma'am."

A scream came from the direction of the cellar and Polly's eyes shot open. "*Go!*" she urged Danil.

He hesitated for the briefest moment, patting his pockets as if looking for something he could use as a weapon. The only knife he had was for cutting meat, not slicing enemies open.

Polly shoved her dagger at him and he took it gratefully. She gave him a sharp nod and he took off running.

Danil was soon out of the range of Polly's vision. Though he was now blanketed in darkness, he knew the rough direction he needed to head in. He tripped over something and sprawled in the dirt but was back up and running before he lost his momentum.

A moment later he saw himself running down the street through the eyes of a woman who was watching him. "Thank the Bitch for that," he muttered to himself.

He jumped from mind to mind, piggybacking the visions of the villagers who watched him run, hearts in their throats. The slimmest sparks of hope were beginning to flicker.

Even as he ran he was aware of the attempts to stifle the unfamiliar feeling. These people had been so long without hope that they barely recognized it when they saw it...and they reflexively shied away from it.

"You people really need to lighten the fuck up," Danil gasped.

He came to a sliding stop at the end of the lane behind two remnant who were pounding on the door of the tiny stone building. Two trembling men stood behind them and before Danil could make it over to them one of the men hefted a rock. It caught a remnant right in the middle of its back.

The beast turned, red eyes flashing angrily as it growled. The villager who'd thrown the rock took one nervous step backward and hunched.

Danil could sense that he had no idea what to do next but he refused to back down despite the fear gnawing at his gut.

His companion edged away and a second later, a rock flew from his fist too. This one smacked against the door of the cellar, missing the other remnant's head by inches.

Both men now had the attention of one of the Skrim-controlled remnant and they exchanged a quick glance before taking off running. One of them hurtled past Danil, his eyes opening in shock when he saw the mystic.

Danil neatly stepped between the fleeing man and the remnant who was chasing him. He twirled Polly's dagger around one finger, and instead of ducking beneath the remnant's clawed hand Danil jumped into the air, grunting as the remnant slammed its head into his torso.

When the remnant's arms encircled his waist Danil tensed and thrust downward, stabbing the knife through both the Skrim and the spinal cord of its remnant host.

The Skrim was silent, but the remnant let out a slight gurgle. Both creatures were dead in seconds.

Danil hit the ground as the suddenly-limp arms ceased holding his weight. He shoved the body off and stumbled to his feet.

Absentmindedly wiping the knife on his pants, Danil used his borrowed sight to seek out the other man who had fled with a remnant on his tail. They were nowhere to be seen, but Danil called out anyway.

"Run to me! To me!"

Danil spun toward a nearby building. A woman hid behind it, and he could see his own image drift in and out of her sight when she pulled back behind the wall, then peeked again.

"You! Over here, now." The woman stuck her head out, threw a nervous glance down the road, and darted over to him.

"I need your eyes," Danil said.

The woman started back, terrified. "My...eyes?"

Danil felt a brush of amusement. "Bitch's oath, woman, I'm not going to take them out of your head. I just need you to show me where to go."

The woman's fear didn't subside. *Understandably*, Danil thought. He'd asked her to leave her safe hiding spot to lead him to the very beasts trying to kill her. To her credit, she didn't refuse.

Danil grabbed her hand and they ran in the direction the last remnant had gone.

"Your name is Annabeth?" Danil asked as they flew across the tiny village.

Annabeth almost tripped in shock. "How did you know?"

"I read minds." At her look of shock and awe, Danil added, "Did I forget to mention that?"

This time Annabeth did trip. She was saved from landing face-first on the rough road by a quick jerk on her arm. Danil turned to her with a grin.

Annabeth had noticed the way the strange visitor's eyes had glowed earlier but had convinced herself that because they weren't remnant-red he wasn't dangerous.

Learning that he had magic, though, made her stomach twist...and his hand on her arm only made it worse.

"I'm not going to hurt you," Danil said carefully, releasing his grip once she had found her feet.

Annabeth's mind raced to catch up with the revelation. "I...know. I mean, you wouldn't be here killing the remnant otherwise, would you?"

She tore her eyes from the strange man beside her and came face to face with a pair that glowed bright red. Annabeth skidded to a stop but it was too late—they already had the remnant's attention.

Danil flung an arm out and pushed her backward.

"Even if I can't see I can still fight." Danil shot her a quick glance. "If you want to run, do it while he's distracted. Otherwise, stay out of sight but watch if you can."

Annabeth jerked her head in a nod. "I'll stay."

The words fell out of her mouth before she realized she was going to say them. Her stomach spasmed again as she realized she had just agreed to help this stranger—the one with magic, for Bitch's sake!—fight the crazed beast in front of them.

Danil stepped forward and crouched in a defensive stance with Polly's dagger outstretched. He waggled the fingers of his other hand to gesture the remnant closer.

"Come on, you big baby. What are you waiting for?" he taunted. Every sense was tuned to the remnant's smell, its sound, and the pattern of the breeze it blocked. He didn't want to be caught in the dark if Annabeth changed her mind at the last moment.

The remnant sneered and lunged at him. Danil braced to meet the attack, then reeled back in shock as it lunged not at him but at Annabeth.

Annabeth's head snapped back as the remnant punched her in the jaw. Her vision swam, and her last conscious thought was that if she didn't stay awake, Danil wouldn't be able to see. *If he can't see, how will he save me?*

Danil roared in fury as the remnant snatched up his victim and sprinted away. Danil chased him, the sound of uneven feet thumping on the ground his only guide.

The remnant pulled away, its supernatural speed giving it even more of an edge than the simple ability of sight. Desperation filled the mystic.

Pain flared in Annabeth's jaw, piercing the dark shroud that clouded her mind. She was vaguely aware of being jolted, but her thoughts were centered on the pain

I'm sorry to wake you, a voice said inside her head. *But I really need you to pay attention. Now...when I tell you to run, RUN!*

In her foggy state, Annabeth didn't even question why a strange woman might be giving instructions inside her head. The urgency that filled the imaginary voice pierced the haze, though Annabeth struggled to free her mind from the grip of sleep.

She was bounced roughly, then her captor suddenly stopped.

Her stomach lurched as the world flipped upside down; whoever had been carrying her dumped her roughly on the ground.

Darkness clouded the edges of her vision again as her face slammed into the ground and pain exploded, but this time the darkness didn't win.

Something held it back, pushing away the blissful relief of unconsciousness. A thin wavering groan escaped Annabeth's lips.

Run. The voice, loud and insistent, echoed in her head. *Run!*

Even through her agony Annabeth sensed the urgency of what she was being asked to do. She might be in pain, but she was alive—and whoever her new friend was, it seemed the woman wanted her to stay that way.

Annabeth rolled to her hands and feet and pushed herself up, then ran.

Her legs wobbled, but she stumbled toward the trees, pushing branches and leaves out of the way as she hurled herself into the forest.

Just as her knees were about to give way a man stepped out from behind a tree. Blonde hair flopped over his face, and his finely-sculpted body was the last thing she saw before she collapsed into his arms. Her eyes drifted closed, but before she sank back into a stupor Marcus heard her whisper something.

"Please don't eat me."

Marcus chuckled. "It's okay. I've already had breakfast." He scooped the girl up and carried her over to the horses, then looked around and realized there was nowhere to put her down except for the cold ground.

Although he considered doing so, he thought Julianne might tear him a new one if she saw the bruised and bleeding girl they had just rescued discarded on the ground like a bit of rubbish.

Marcus juggled the limp body in his arms to get a better grip.

"Hurry up, Jules. She's kinda heavy." Realizing what he had said, Marcus counted his lucky stars that Julianne hadn't been in his head at the time.

Don't count on it.

Shaking her head at Marcus's thoughtless comment, Julianne brought her attention to the scene before her. She stood on the edge of Kells and leaves rustled on branches swaying in a gentle breeze in the forest behind the town at her back.

The town would have been picturesque, except for the ugly-ass monster that ruined the view.

"What? You didn't expect to see me?" Julianne twirled her staff, bringing it to a stop with one end pointed directly at her opponent.

The remnant apparently didn't want to waste time on niceties. It lunged at her lightning-fast, teeth bared in a furious growl.

Julianne twisted out of its way and flicked her staff between its ankles, and the remnant fell. It rolled on its knees, then leapt toward her again.

This time the staff caught it in the face; the wet crack of solid wood against soft cartilage and bone made her grimace.

Its head snapped back and the remnant stumbled and went down again. It refused to give up, though.

Face pulped and bleeding and breath coming in bubbling gasps, the remnant pulled itself onto all fours once more.

"Just fuckin' die already, ye prick." Garrett flung his axe, then ducked the spurt of blood that erupted from the remnant's neck.

Julianne danced out of the way as the head rolled past her.

"About bloody time," Danil exclaimed, hands on hips. "Where's Annabeth?"

"She's with Marcus," Julianne replied. She winced. "She's going to be in a world of pain when she wakes up, though."

"Speaking of pain," Polly called as she hobbled up the path behind them. "I'm starting to wish we'd brought a druid with us."

Julianne ran over to the girl and offered her an arm to lean on.

"Why is it that when *I* offer you help you get offended," Danil asked, "but when Julianne does it she's the nicest person in the world?"

"Because yer a man," Garrett told him firmly. "And cuz yer a man, yer destined ta never understand. At least I never did, in all me years o' bein' a man."

"I thought you would get a pass, being only half a man," Danil quipped.

"'Half a man?' Ye can come back ta me on that one when ye've caught up ta me in kills." Garrett sniggered and held up the haft of his axe.

He drew out a small pocket knife and scored a line in the handle, then ran his finger down a series of similar notches and turned to Danil. "How many did *ye* get today? Twelve? Because unless ye got twelve, ye still haven't caught up."

Danil scowled and turned his back on the rearick, sidling over to Polly.

"How's the ankle?"

Polly gave him a brave grin. "Feels like someone took a bite out of me."

She lifted her leg and Danil saw that the rough bandage she had applied was now soaked in blood.

"Doesn't look so bad," he said sympathetically. "It might hurt like hell, but I think it'll heal all right."

"The bastard ruined my shoes," Polly griped.

"When we get back home I'll buy you all the shoes in Tahn." Danil grinned, expecting her to be pleased.

Instead, Polly scowled. "I hope you mean Muir. You can't even buy nice *boots* in Tahn."

Danil hastily backtracked. "Yes, Muir. That was exactly what I meant." *How the hell am I supposed to know where to buy women's boots?* he sent to Julianne.

He caught the grin his fellow mystic tried to hide. *It's just one of those things.*

CHAPTER FOURTEEN

"You know I'm right," Tansy said, hands planted firmly on her hips.

"You're right that it will *help*," Bastian replied. "But I don't know if that will help enough to make it worth the effort. We're in the middle of a war, Tansy! We've got refugees flooding in from all across Irth and resources are tight. The people who live here have already taken on so much more work than they should have ever had to, and now you're asking them to host a celebration? I just don't think it's the right time for it."

"It's *exactly* the right time for it."

Bastian jumped and turned to the newcomer. "Annie! I didn't expect to see you down this way today."

Annie shook her head at him. "I go wherever I'm needed most."

Bastian wondered if he was right to feel a pang of guilt for assuming she would be anywhere else. Despite their successful defeat of the remnant the previous day, the newcomers to the tiny village were clearly still struggling with their situation. Bette's idea to have them fight the remnant had certainly helped to lift their spirits, but there was still work to be done...and Annie was there to do it.

The old woman had been baking up a storm, bringing sweet and savory gifts to the Hall where the refugees slept and taking it to sites where Bastian had put building crews to work erecting new accommodation for the growing number of Tahn residents.

"So...you're in favor of it?" Bastian asked dubiously. "You really think we have the resources to host a celebration in the middle of all this?"

Annie gave a firm nod. "You did it for us once before," she reminded him. "And I know my people. Everyone in this city was better off for it. After you lot swept in here and took over, it was good to see that you were confident enough of your eventual success to hold a party."

Bastian shuffled uncomfortably. "We didn't *take over*, did we?"

"Not in a bad way," Annie reassured him. "You saw we were struggling and filled in some gaps. You managed to do it without stepping on any toes, and you made sure that as soon as the immediate danger was over one of our own could step up to the plate."

"If Annie's given her blessing, does that mean I have yours too?" Tansy asked, fluttering her eyelashes at Bastian.

He groaned. "Fine. And I'm guessing you wouldn't be asking me if you hadn't already cleared it with Francis?"

"Of course I did," Tansy scolded. "He said he thought it was a wonderful idea, but that I'd have one hell of a time convincing you of that."

Bastian sighed in defeat. "You could have said that to start with! He's in charge around here, not me. Why are you asking my permission?"

"I'm not," Tansy replied. "I'm asking if you'll perform for it."

Bastian yelped. "Me? Perform?"

Tansy nodded confidently. "It was Francis' idea, actually. We want you to do that story-weaving thing again, but instead of the tale you told about Bethany Anne, Francis suggested you should make it about Julianne. Well, and Marcus and the others, too. Tell the refugees we have a group of heroes traipsing around the countryside rescuing people. It'll give them hope that those they've left behind and those they have lost might still be rescued and brought home."

Bastian hissed out a breath through his teeth, then nodded. He was certainly capable of weaving story images, though everyone else seemed to think more of his ability than he did. Still, if Tansy and Francis thought it would help he would do it.

"I'm glad that's settled," Annie said. "Now, we need to plan food and seating, and we should give the whole thing a festive air. Those people are miserable enough. They need some brightness in their lives."

"Yes!" Tansy exclaimed. "I've got a big pile of beautiful cloth from Tessa. It's meant to be used for dresses for the women and girls, but we can use it just for that evening to provide some color."

Bastian slid his chair back with a squawk and stood. "You ladies seem to have this well in hand," he said. "I need to go see Angelica. She's been pestering me for a meeting and I can't put it off any longer. Let me know what I need to do to help and I'll make it happen."

He paused on his way out the door to plant a firm kiss on Tansy's lips. "You call Julianne a hero," he mumbled in her ear. "You're just as much of a hero as she is. Everyone here can see that, and no one more than me."

Tansy blushed and gave him a half-hearted slap on the shoulder. "Oh, go on, you. Flattery will get you everywhere. Go…do your work, and make sure you're back here by early afternoon!"

"We'll make sure we have a nice long list of things for you to do when you get back," Annie said with a grin.

Once Bastian had left, Tansy and Annie fell to planning the upcoming celebration.

"We'll put Tessa in charge of organizing the decorations," Annie said. "She's got a lot to do already, but she's good at delegating—and if we left her out of this she would skin us alive."

"With all that baking you've been doing, Annie, do you think you could handle a bit more?" Tansy asked. "That cheesecake you brought down the other day was just incredible."

Annie scowled. "That was for the refugees."

Tansy giggled. "I was on the serving line. I didn't eat any, but you can be damn sure I licked my fingers when I was done. I've never tasted anything so amazing. It was lucky there was none left by then or I'd have stolen it and eaten it all."

Annie's scowl softened. "I suppose that's all right then. And yes, I've got enough left that I can whip up another. I can bring that and a tray of those little caramel tarts and a few dozen plain rolls to go with whatever meat we can find." Annie jerked her head down in a nod, a gesture Tansy had come to realize meant Annie had added something to her personal to-do list. The woman had a mind like a steel trap; there was no chance of Annie promising to do something and not following through.

"Beautiful," Tansy said. "I'll go find some of the men. I'm sure Bette can spare someone to go out on a hunt. We'll need a nice fat beast to feed us all, and we'll want to start roasting it first thing tomorrow morning if it's to be tender and juicy by nightfall." Tansy stood to go and asked, "What else do I need to do?"

"Well, if you don't come up with something for that boy of yours to do he'll be feeling awfully left out." Annie gave Tansy a knowing look.

"Oh, I'll have plenty for him to help with." Tansy giggled. "Don't you worry about that."

Tansy skipped out, excited that her plans were coming to fruition. She jogged through the main street of Tahn, waving at the small groups of people she passed on her way to the watchtower. By the time she'd scaled the ladder, she had a wide grin plastered on her face.

"Ye look like ye just rolled out of bed with yer man," Bette pointed out with a sly smile when she saw Tansy.

"That was hours ago. This is better than that anyway," Tansy told her.

"If there's anythin' better 'n that, yer lad's not doing 'is job right." Bette sniggered. "Anyway, what's got ye so happy?"

"We're having a party. A festival! A celebration of all that is good in the world, with food and dancing and lots and lots of alcohol." Tansy angled a finger toward Bette. "I need you to provide me with the food. Well, not *you* exactly... Do you have anyone free to go catch a fat beast?"

Bette sighed. "Sounds ta me like they don't have a choice. Luckily fer yer festival, Francis already asked me ta send out a huntin' party today. Sharne is leadin' it, but yer welcome ta go with 'em if ye want."

Tansy shook her head, frowning. "I'll be far too busy to go, but otherwise I would. I haven't been out for ages!"

"Feelin' a bit closed in, are ye?" Bette asked sympathetically.

Tansy nodded. "I know that I'm needed here, and I'm definitely being kept busy. But I'm looking forward to when this is all over."

Tansy's eyes drifted from Bette to the watchtower. From here she could see all the way to the forest. "I can't *wait* until life returns to normal. Dinner at home, days spent roaming the countryside."

Bette scoffed. "Even before the shite hit the fan, I woulda never picked ye as a roamin'-the-countryside kinda lass."

"I'm not," Tansy said with a weary sigh. "But as soon as you say I can't do a thing, it's all I want. I only went out on hunts once a week or so, but Bitch's oath, I still miss it."

Bette turned her gaze toward the horizon. "I know the feelin'. I spend most o' me time inside the city anyway, but I *do* miss the odd adventure. Even when the remnant come I'm usually stuck up here givin' directions instead o' down there with an axe in me hand, takin' off heads an' spillin' blood all over the ground." She sighed again.

"And *that* is exactly why we need to have this celebration," Tansy declared. "As a reminder that even though we can't have everything we want, we're alive and well. We have plenty of food and the ability to fight back against our enemies. I think it's good to be reminded of that every now and then."

"Ye've got that right," Bette said. "Ye'd best be off, lass. Sharne wanted ta move out by mid-morning, so if ye want ta make sure they don't come back till they catch somethin' worthy o' yer feast, ye'll need ta let them know before they leave."

"I'll do that," Tansy said, heading toward the ladder. "We're planning to have some entertainment too," she called over her shoulder. "If any of your boys and girls would like to put on a show, let me know."

"I'll do that!" Bette called after her.

CHAPTER FIFTEEN

Bastian whirled Tansy around the dance floor, feeling the heat of the early-summer evening prickle his skin. Tansy's cheeks were flushed and her forehead was beaded with sweat.

The song came to an end and old Jessop put his fiddle down, gasping for breath. Despite his age he had played like a man possessed, stomping his feet and twirling in time to the music that drifted from his ancient instrument.

"I need a drink," Tansy wheezed when they came to a halt.

"Me too," Bastian admitted. He took her hand after wiping the sweat from his own against his pants and led her to the table where Tamara waited expectantly with a bowl of punch, ladle hovering.

"Two?" Tamara asked, dipping the spoon into the deep bowl and pouring the fruity concoction into the brass cup. She repeated the action, then handed the drinks over and grinned. "Looks like you're having fun tonight."

"Isn't it amazing?" Tansy sighed and her eyes sparkled with excitement as she surveyed the room.

"It is, thanks to you." Tamara gave the younger girl a reassuring smile, then sighed whimsically. "I imagine there will be an even bigger celebration once the school opens." She cocked a questioning eyebrow at Bastian.

Irritated, he took a gulp of punch and almost choked on it. After he'd coughed and spluttered for a moment he grimaced. "The school *will* open. Tamara, I know you're frustrated with the delay, but—"

"Yes, yes, I know." Tamara passed him a cloth napkin and nodded at the spot where he'd dribbled on his shirt. "It's just that there's no point in my heading back to Arcadia now. I'm eager to find my place, and as helpful as Annie has been, it seems I won't have one until then."

"I'm sorry, Tamara, but there's just nothing I can do about that right now. I have other priorities." Bastian heard someone say his name and looked around distractedly. "Oh, that's Mary. Uhh…" He looked around for a safe place to leave his cup.

Tansy plucked it from his hands and kissed his cheek. "Go."

He hurried off. After wondering briefly what she was going to do with two drinks, Tansy bolted one and set the other inside it. Pleased—and just a little fuzzy in the head from the quick dose of alcohol—she smiled at Tamara.

"Your passion is teaching?" she asked.

Tamara nodded. "I didn't last long at the Academy. My ideas were too…progressive for the Chancellor. Amelia did offer me a place when she stepped up but filled it after I declined. I should have said yes, but I let my pride get in the way."

Tansy shrugged. "So?"

Tamara snorted. "*So?* Girl, when was the last time *you* turned down the one position that would allow you to serve your given purpose in the world? I know it's my own stupid fault, but—"

"No," Tansy interrupted. "I mean, *so* you don't have a fancy building to teach in. Do you really need one?" She waved a hand at the dancing crowd. "How many of those refugee kids do you think can read? You want to teach? *Teach!* Teach what's needed wherever you can. Don't wait for the school. Just do it!"

Tamara blinked slowly, her mouth ajar, and a moment later she sucked in a gasp of air as if she'd forgotten to breathe.

"You're welcome," Tansy said smartly. She grinned at the grey-haired teacher and dipped a low curtsy. As she whirled away to find her lover, she almost didn't hear the hurried 'thank you' that rang behind her. Almost…

She found Bastian still talking to Mary. The tavern owner quickly excused herself when she saw Tansy coming, firmly instructing Bastian to stop finding excuses to work at a party.

Jessop handed the fiddle to Lewis, who was striking up a tune. The dance floor filled again; Tahn residents mingling with refugees, all smiling and laughing as they danced. Tansy pulled Bastian away, though. Her head was properly swimming now, and she needed to put something in her stomach to settle it.

"Let's find something to eat."

She dragged him past Tamara, who gave an excited wave, and over to the long table that had been covered with platters of meat and vegetables earlier. Cooked over a low fire since early morning, the tantalizing aroma of the fat stag had ensured it was devoured quickly. Now all that remained was the carcass and a few pieces of cold meat.

Dora caught Tansy's disappointed glance at the table. "Not still hungry, are you?" she asked with a laugh. "I hope you are. Annie just came in to say she's about to clear that away to put out dessert."

Tansy's eyes shot open and she nudged Bastian. "You know what that means, don't you?"

Clenching his stomach to quell the flutter of nerves, Bastian nodded. Tansy had only reminded him about forty-seven times that he was to take the stage between dinner and dessert to craft his story about the hero Julianne and her intrepid band of adventurers.

"You look terrified." Tansy giggled. "Why? You've done this before!"

He nodded. "I have, but that was more a spur-of-the-moment thing. I didn't realize how much people would like it, and now there's all this pressure to do it again...but better." He ran his fingers through his hair anxiously. "I know, it doesn't make any sense at all."

"You're right," Tansy agreed. "Not one bit of sense. But the sooner you get it over and done with, the sooner you can stop worrying about it and take me out on the floor for another dance."

That made Bastian smile, and he tugged on his robes and stood tall. "How do I look?"

Tansy clicked her tongue and shook her head. "You mean you're not changing first? Bastian, you really need to get some new clothes. You wear those same robes *everywhere*."

Wincing, Bastian replied, "I thought you loved me no matter what I look like?"

Tansy rolled her eyes dramatically. "*I* love you, but half the people here don't even know you. This is a party, Bastian! You're supposed to be going up there to present a spectacle, and you can't do that in this ratty old white robe."

A sly grin spread over Bastian's face. "I might be wearing a ratty old white robe, but who says anyone will know?"

Before Tansy's eyes, Bastian's robes—which were really more grey than white—began to sparkle. The discoloration of age disappeared, replaced by the purest glowing white she had ever seen.

Tansy glanced at his face, unsurprised to see his eyes glowing the same color as his new robes. "Cheater," she said with a grin.

She leaned in for a kiss, and as she pulled back a line of deep-blue trim embroidered with gold flowers wound its way down the edges of his robe. Her eyes followed it and when she got to his feet, his creased grey boots turned black and shiny as if they were brand-new.

Tansy stepped back and ran her eyes over his attire, then grinned. "Now *that's* what I call well-dressed!"

Bastian returned the smile. "I'm glad you like it, but now I have to go do my thing."

As the only mystic left in town, Bastian felt it was his duty to put on a show Tahn would never forget. Though Danil's absence compounded his anxiety about the presentation he was about to give, he thought he would be able to pull it off. That was, if he could make it past the eyes staring at him intently as he climbed onto the small stage.

Seeing Bastian approach, Lewis quickly wrapped up his tune and bowed deeply.

"Ladies and gentlemen, may I present Bastian, mystic extraordinaire!" Lewis thrust his arms wide, signaling the crowd to applaud.

Bastion resisted the urge to tug at his collar and channeled just a little of his magic into controlling his emotions. Illusion firmly in place and nerves settled into a confident calm, Bastian stepped forward.

"Ladies and gentlemen," Bastian called, tweaking his spell so that every face in the room turned his way, caught by the man in white who seemed to glow in the amber light of the flickering lanterns that filled the room. "Tonight I bring you a gift. The gift of knowledge. The gift of a story as true as it is unbelievable."

Bastian muttered a word and waved his hands for effect. The hand gestures were unrelated to his magic, but Zoe had once told him people liked it. He stepped back as an image formed in front of him.

It was a woman with brown hair and glowing white eyes. She wore a robe as bright and pristine as the illusion made his own and held a long white staff. The image showed Julianne as he remembered her—tall, proud, and commanding, yet kind.

Her posture had the strength and confidence of a woman who knew she would win any battle she entered, and yet her face held the softness of someone who would never hesitate to stop and give comfort to a child in the street.

"Julianne, Master of the Heights." Bastion called. He had to pause to allow the smattering of applause to die down. To know her was to respect her, so the response to her name warmed Bastian's heart.

"Julianne, the great Leader of the Mystics, Warrior in the fight against the Arcadian dictator Adrien, Liberator of Tahn, and Savior of Lord George of Muir."

The cheers rose again and Bastion grinned with excitement. He moved his hands and beside Julianne a blonde man appeared, clad in armor and holding a staff as well. The stick was shaped oddly and sported a bright, glowing jewel in one side.

"Marcus, the Warrior—"

"And a right good lover, if he snagged the Master Mystic," someone yelled from the crowd. Bastion stifled a snort of laughter as giggles ran through his audience.

"And what a pair they make," Bastion agreed, acknowledging the relationship between Julianne and Marcus.

"They were joined by another couple destined to save the world—Danil the Blind and Polly the Righteous...and by their side, Garrett the Rearick."

As he named each member of the absent party their image appeared. Bastion knew they probably weren't quite true to life; they stood a little taller and the faces looked to be carved from stone. No, rather than a realistic depiction of each of his friends, they appeared as he saw them in his mind. Perfect. Immutable. Powerful, honorable, and kind.

"This brave band of warriors travels the countryside as we speak, searching for unprotected towns—like Tahn once was." Bastion ran his eyes over the crowd as he waited for them to fall silent again. "Those who lived here then know the transformation this town has undergone. From a sleepy farm village to a haven of safety and a beacon of strength in dark times. From farmers and crafters to warriors and providers for the region. This is the change Julianne and her group will help implement across the land."

"She goes to save the world from the alien beasts!" a voice called.

"They go to rescue the innocent and destroy the remnant!" came another call.

Bastian nodded. "She goes to liberate people from whatever enemies they face, but primarily she goes to close the rifts; the cracks in the sky that let this vile enemy through. An enemy who has roused the remnant and sent them to ravage the countryside. She goes to save the lives under threat from the Skrima, and to restore freedom and peace."

Bastian waved a hand again and the images changed. Instead of five people standing tall, they now posed instead for battle. The audience watched as Julianne rammed her sword into a lumbering Skrim and gasped as Danil and Polly danced around a remnant, stabbing and slicing until the beast was brought to its knees. They cheered Marcus and Garrett as each faced a sea of remnant, Marcus shooting his amphorald-powered rifle and Garrett hurling an axe, then spinning to draw a sword.

The audience hollered, shouted, and squealed as the battling heroes took injuries while dealing death to their enemies.

"Together, this team of warriors will free Irth of this scourge!"

The five separate images merged into one, representing the battle Bastian knew was coming. He had seen Skrima-controlled remnant in a transmission from Julianne, so he showed this to those who watched.

The glowing, swirling battle scene showed Julianne and her friends fighting a horde of possessed remnant, flicking away attacks and dodging old and rusted weapons. Bastian showed them fighting...and winning.

The illusory battle soon ended and Julianne turned back to

face the crowd, piles of dead at her feet flickering into wisps of smoke as Bastian struggled to hold the image.

He flooded the room with pride and hope. He made them believe that, against all odds, good would triumph over evil. He knew the effect wouldn't last, but right now they needed what little he could give.

He knew there was a chance, however small, that the story he had told tonight would take wings. It would spread throughout the region as rumors and fireside tales, traveling the lands to give hope to terrified strangers and desperate villages waiting for rescue. He felt the weight of the responsibility and hoped he had lived up to it.

The crowd erupted into cheers, startling Bastian so much so that he jumped. *That* wasn't an emotion he had crafted. Wild joy and heartfelt adulation filled the crowd as his images faded.

Bastian sought Tansy. Almost hidden in the crowd, she stared back at him, eyes wide and filmed with tears.

I love you, she mouthed. *You did well.*

Bastian's heart swelled as he stepped off the stage and made his way toward his lover through the press of bodies on the dance floor. He could tell by their faces that he really had made a difference. The townspeople and the refugees exuded new purpose and determination, and the underlying fear and despair had all but disappeared.

A shrill bell pierced the babble of conversation that filled the hall and a thick silence blanketed the room.

"Attack!" Carey yelled, confirming the bell's warning.

The silence was quickly filled with babbling voices and the clatter of movement. To Bastian's surprise the reaction was not one of fear, but of excitement.

"To the wall!" an elderly lady at Bastian's elbow called. She shot him a cheeky glance. "You gave us a taste of the fight. Don't tell me you expect us to stay behind now?"

"Maybe you'll get one of your own this time, Esme, instead of trying to claim my kill," an elderly man remarked to the woman he'd been dancing with.

"That was *my* spear sticking out of his belly, Arnold." The woman smacked his shoulder roughly, though she grinned with excitement as she did so. "And don't you be telling anyone otherwise. You're as useless on the battlefield as you are in the kitchen!"

Arnold grumbled but gave up his argument. He grabbed Esme's hands and pulled her toward the door. "Well if we *both* kill one this time there won't be any arguing. Hurry up or there'll be none left for us!"

Bastian looked for Tansy in the crowd. She had jumped on top of a long table, and was gingerly stepping across the mess of plates and cups to make her way toward him. She hopped lightly to the ground and ran over.

"I thought I was going to get trampled in the stampede," she said. "I've never seen a bunch of geriatric villagers run so fast toward a fight. What did Bette *do* to them yesterday?"

"She showed them what they were capable of," Bastian responded with a grin. "Are you coming? I want to see this for myself."

"Wouldn't miss it for the world." Like the older couple who had left earlier, Tansy grabbed Bastian's hand and dragged him toward the exit, jostling past the people hurrying to find weapons and make their way to the wall.

"I hope you don't expect to find a spear," Bastian called to Tansy. "At this rate there'll be none left."

"Forget the spears; there won't be any remnant left to throw them at. I don't think our skills will be needed. I just want to watch."

They hurried after the crowd of eager fighters but stopped at the bottom of the watchtower ladder in dismay.

"No more, no more!" Bette yelled from above. "The wall's at

capacity. Any more bodies up here and the whole thing will come tumblin' down."

"Then open the gate," an old woman called, and Bastian winced. She had to be at least in her seventies and leaned heavily on her cane

"Not a damned chance, ye silly old goat," Bette responded. "If ye want ta fight the remnant, turn up ta weapons trainin'. I'm not lettin' any o' ye out there until ye've shown ye can hold yer own in a fight."

Bastian's heart fell at the dismayed grumbling around him. "We can't fight," he called, "but we can watch."

Bastian pulled himself up onto the bottom rung of the ladder so he was standing just above the others. He let out a slow breath, hoping he had the energy left to master the spell he was about to cast. He muttered a word and his eyes shone.

Atop the wall, Sharne grinned at the familiar presence in her mind. She scanned the battlefield, obeying Bastian's silent request to give him the best view in the house.

Back on the ground, squeals of delight drowned out the noise of battle as the image sprang to life. The inside defensive wall now acted like a screen, displaying the view Sharne was sharing. Instead of a towering wall, those watching saw a steep drop and a horde of remnant in the distance. Their movements were illuminated by the brightly shining moon and the lanterns that dotted the wall surrounding the village.

"Look, someone threw a spear already!" a young girl called.

"Waste of a bloody weapon," another yelled. "Don't they know they have to wait until the enemy is in range?"

As the remnant drew closer conversation increased, dotted by the occasional yell of advice from the ground to the fighters on the wall.

"Throw it harder!"

"*Aim* the bloody thing before you let it go."

"Look, there's one trying to sneak off to the side"

The sly remnant who had tried to peel off from the rest of his group was quickly speared and the audience hooted in joy. Any meaning in the babble of conversation was lost in the throes of excitement.

Tansy gave Bastian an exuberant squeeze around the middle. The earlier celebratory mood had only increased in the face of the unexpected attack; the people who had arrived in Tahn broken and afraid were now fighting back.

Those without spears wielded a more powerful weapon—hope. They held it high and proud, and thrust it into the faces of the enemy with yells of delight and cries of encouragement.

The remnant quickly realized there would be no penetrating this well-protected village. One and then another began to run, their retreat followed by the bulk of the attackers.

They didn't get far. Thanks to Bette's foresight in providing as many weapons as could possibly be made, the villagers and refugees were able to pin the fleeing remnant to the dirt by raining spears from the sky.

"Stop!" Bette's panicked holler cut through the din. "They're all dead! Stop wastin' me bloody weapons, ye fools!"

Nervous laughter spread through those on top of the wall. Bastian wondered how long it would take for the newcomers to fear Bette's tongue-lashings more than whatever the enemy might present at the gate. It certainly hadn't taken her soldiers long to realize that the stout young woman commanded far more power than the rabble they fought.

Bastian let the image of the now-quiet battlefield fade way. "Mac, open the gates," he called weakly.

The small posse of soldiers who had gone out to face the enemy entered to the cheers and handshakes of those waiting for them.

Lewis caught Bastian's eye and frowned. "We didn't even get a kill in," he complained, "but they're treating us like heroes."

"You've killed enough of the bastards over the last year to deserve the title," Bastian assured him kindly.

Lewis shrugged again and wandered off into the crowd, enduring the claps on the back and the occasional grandma who swooped in to kiss him on the cheek.

The crowd slowly dispersed and people began to wander back to the Hall.

"Not twenty minutes ago we were facing an attack by a horde of remnant," Tansy said, "and now everyone is heading in for dessert. Not an outcome I ever expected."

"You and me both," Bastian said. "But if we don't move fast, that cheesecake will run out faster than the remnant did."

"Then what are you waiting for?" Tansy asked, yanking his arm to hurry him up.

Bastian trotted back toward the Hall and the celebration that had already resumed inside. Idly, he wondered what Julianne and the rest of his friends were up to on the road. He felt almost guilty for filling his belly with Annie's cheesecake, knowing that Julianne would likely be living on hard jerky and old bread.

CHAPTER SIXTEEN

Julianne gratefully accepted the bowl of stew in one hand and a warm, fresh bread roll in the other.

"What did you add?" Marcus asked through a mouthful of food. "This has spices I didn't bring with me. I don't think I've even *tasted* them before."

"I'm glad you like it," Megan said. The young redhead had introduced herself as Jackson's youngest daughter, and apparently, she'd been in charge of preparing their meal. "It's an herb that grows like a weed around here. Tastes just fine...until it's the only damn thing in town left to flavor food with. After tasting it every day for three months, it makes you start to wonder if flavoring your meals with cow dung might be nicer."

Marcus winced in sympathy. "Well, as someone who is trying it for the first time, it definitely tastes better than that stuff."

"The lad's right; it *is* a good feed. We really can't thank ye enough." Garrett clapped a hand over his mouth to catch the spray of food that flew out when he spoke. It didn't seem to bother him—he licked his lips, pulled the chunk of potato from his beard, and popped it in his mouth with an expression of joy.

"Garrett's right," Julianne said. "We know you're struggling to provide for your own people, let alone feeding us."

"You seem to be forgetting that it was you who provided the meat," Jackson reminded her. "We just added a few ingredients to fill it out and threw in a bit of herb. We figured you wouldn't be as sick of it as we are."

"Are you really going to take us with you?" Megan asked quietly. "Somewhere safe? I don't even remember what it's like to go to bed and not have to wonder if I'll still be alive in the morning."

Julianne's face creased with sympathy. "We *will* take you with us—all of you. We won't abandon you, and we won't leave you anywhere we can't be sure you're completely safe, even if that means you have to come all the way back to Tahn with us."

"We'd even take ye back ta the Arcadian Valley." Garrett wiped some gravy from his mouth before continuing, "Hell of a trick that'd be! Ye'd have ta cross the Madlands; a place the remnant call their own. Not ta mention the mountain!" Garrett's eyes shone as he remembered his home. He raised a hand and slowly drew it across the sky as he described the place he'd grown up.

"Imagine a mountain stretching so far inta the sky the top is tipped with clouds."

The villagers nodded, and more than one darted a glance at the nearby range. It was tipped with clouds for most of the day, but they let him continue.

"When yer there on a stormy day, yer livin' right in the guts o' the clouds. On those days ye can look out the window and not see the far side o' the street. Ye have ta be careful on days like that." He opened his eyes wide, warning etched on his face. "Ye can be walkin' on the road, puttin' one foot in front o' the other; as blind as Danil here without 'is magic. One wrong step—" Garrett slammed his palms on the dirt. "Splat! Hell of a fall, and I guarantee ye wouldn't survive!"

Julianne's eyes scanned the faces around her, worried that

Garrett's somber warning might be too much for their already fear-worn companions. However, after what these people had gone through, a quick death from dropping off a cliff seemed benign in comparison.

Garrett continued his story, moving on to talk about the sheer majesty of the Heights. He told them of the beautiful views on a clear day, the bright stars that seemed to hang within arm's reach, and the pristine blankets of snow that covered the mountains through most of winter. His speech was so heartfelt that Julianne found herself warding off a pang of homesickness.

Marcus rested a hand on Julianne's shoulder. His face was creased with sympathy, so she quickly checked his shields to make sure she hadn't been leaking her thoughts to him. Relieved to find them intact, she reached out to Marcus questioningly.

I can read you like a book, Marcus sent to her. *It's written all over your face. You miss the Heights when Garrett talks about them like this.*

Julianne gave a small nod of confirmation. As much as she enjoyed traveling the land, a part of her would always belong at the temple.

"But Julianne can tell ye about that." Garrett looked at Julianne expectantly, and she realized that she had missed whatever he had said.

"Go on, Julianne," Megan prompted. "Tell us about the temple. What's it like?"

A blissful smile touched Julianne's lips and she told them of the grand stone building set into the side of the mountain, built so long ago that it almost looked as if it had risen from the rocks. She told them of the walls that held the heat from the fires to buffer them against the icy winters, and the high ceilings that made even the smallest room seem majestic.

"Our meals are taken in the great hall," she said, closing her eyes and remembering the joy of meeting with her fellow mystics over a hearty feast. "The windows are mottled glass, and they stretch four times as tall as any man. The lanterns are hung from the ceiling, on great chains that can raise them to the ceiling if needed. Our tables are crafted by rearick from ancient trees, sanded and buffed until they're as smooth as glass. The stone floor is streaked with the paint of ancient pictures that wore away and were repainted, then wore away again."

Sharp breaths and cries of delight made Julianne open her eyes. She hadn't realized she had cast the spell, but the image of the great hall of the temple was as perfect as she remembered it. The long tables were filled with white-robed figures, and flickering lanterns made the shadows dance across the walls.

"How did you do that?" Megan asked. "Do you have the same magic Flea has?"

Julianne's heart skipped a beat. "Who is Flea?"

Megan searched the small gathering of people. "It's really Felicity, but everyone calls her Flea—because she's so tiny, you see? Flea? Come here, my love. Show the pretty lady your butterflies."

The girl shuffled from the crowd, pushed forward by an older woman. Julianne guessed she might be thirteen, though her hollow cheeks and skinny legs suggested she might well be younger. The girl's cheeks flushed pink and she turned her head away in embarrassment.

Julianne stood and approached the girl, then crouched in front of her. The child shrank further into herself.

"Flea, I'd really like to see your butterflies." Julianne's eyes glowed a soft white as she whispered something and lifted her gently cupped hand. "Do they look anything like these?" Three butterflies with brilliant blue wings fluttered over to sit on Julianne's fingertips.

Flea's shoulders dropped and she lifted her eyes to Julianne's. Lips still clamped tightly together, she nodded.

"Can you show me?" Julianne asked gently.

Flea nodded. Her eyes took on a similar shine to Julianne's and a butterfly—this one a flickering orange—drifted in on the gentle breeze that brushed past them. A moment later three more appeared, then the air exploded.

A hundred butterflies, each a different color and having a different delicate pattern across its wings, dove and wove and fluttered in a sparkling cloud.

Julianne crowed in delight. She lifted her face and dropped her shields so that she could feel the full effect of Flea's magic. The butterflies' wings tickled her cheeks, and Julianne felt the tiny feet when one landed on her nose. Another settled on her finger and she raised it to examine it closely.

The body wasn't anatomically correct; it was too small, and its wings lacked the delicate structures that provided form to the insect in real life. Instead, this butterfly flew using a sparkling translucent web that had an ethereal quality.

Julianne didn't know if the butterflies' differences were caused by Flea's imagination or simply her lack of knowledge about the finer details of their anatomy. Regardless, the spell demonstrated a talent that was incredibly rare.

"Flea, where is your mother? May I speak to her?"

The butterflies vanished and the suddenly-clear air pressed down on Julianne when Flea turned her head away with a sad, silent frown.

Pain lanced Julianne's heart when she realized how deeply she had stuck her foot in it. "I'm so sorry," she whispered.

"Most of the children here are orphans," Megan explained. "Flea was one of the first to lose her mother. She's...not dealing with it well."

"I don't think there *is* such a thing as dealing well with the loss of a parent," Julianne said quietly. Seeing that Flea had moved out of hearing range, Julianne decided to press on with her inquiry anyway.

"Once we have found you all new homes and gotten you settled in, I would like Flea to come back with me." Julianne raised a hand to forestall any argument. "The temple is the safest place she could possibly be. If she comes back with me, I'll arrange for her to get the training to bring her gift to its full potential."

She didn't mention that Flea, given enough time and adequate training, would be able to hone her power of illusion into something that rivaled even Zoe's. She certainly had the potential to outstrip Julianne, though a strong talent in one area would likely mean she would struggle in others.

That had been one of Julianne's biggest benefits when she was training as a mystic. She was quite strong in all areas, but no particular spell came easier to her than the others. She had to work equally hard in each area of mental magic, so she had avoided the temptation of focusing her time and effort on whatever was easiest.

"It'll have to be up to her," Jackson said from behind Julianne. "You would be taking her away from everything she knows. Bah, after what she's lost, perhaps being away from the constant reminder would be helpful for her."

Julianne nodded. "I understand. I certainly wouldn't want her to come with me if the benefit doesn't outweigh the drawbacks. Megan, would you bring it up with her? It might be easier coming from someone she knows. But do let her know that I won't ask for a decision until this is all over, and I won't pressure her in any way."

Megan considered that for a moment, then nodded. "Very well. So far you've shown good intent. As long as you'll respect her decision if she wants to stay."

Julianne nodded, smiling. "Thank you."

The hour grew late, and one by one their hosts moved into the cottages, carefully closing their doors behind them. Though only a few of the villagers had been brave enough to speak to Julianne and her friends, the air of unwelcome had dissipated.

"We did the right thing by coming back," Polly said. "Didn't we?"

Julianne nodded. "I'm glad you did. I'll rest a lot easier knowing these people are safe. Even traveling the open road with us they will be safer than staying here alone."

"That girl has some pretty powerful magic, Jules," Danil said. "Do you think she'll come back with us? We're in desperate need of recruits, and someone like her would go a long way toward filling the gaps."

Julianne contemplated the prospect. "I hope she does, but at the same time I hate to be the one pulling her away from everything familiar after she's lost so much."

"It won't be easy for her at first," Danil agreed, "but just think, Jules... Where better to heal from that kind of grief than in the temple? They say a grief shared is easier to bear, and the mind links will literally lift that weight from her shoulders if she needs it."

Julianne's mind drifted back to the warm and inviting home she had left and she nodded. "You're right. We certainly have the skills to help her deal with the trauma. And I know that I'm biased, but I really can't think of a nicer place to live."

"It sounds wonderful," Tansy said wistfully. "Danil, I know I said I wanted to travel, but will you take me there one day?" Tansy gave the mystic a nudge. "Danil! Pay attention!"

His eyes, which had flashed white for a moment, cleared. "Sorry," he said with a grin. "I was just talking to Bastian. He wanted to know how we were doing."

"Any news of Tahn?" Julianne asked, trying to stifle a rush of guilt. She knew she had been lax about touching base with Bastian. *Of course, I had a pretty good excuse*, she thought as she looked around the battered village.

"Sounds like they've got it tough," Danil said with a mournful expression. "Late-night parties, dancing, music. I just don't know how he can *stand* it." His eyes sparkled with a wicked mirth and Julianne laughed.

"I'm glad to hear they're doing okay," she said. "I just hope the town is still standing when we get back. I know how the people of Tahn like to celebrate."

As the fire shimmered and died, Julianne's mind was pulled toward a more recent past: the home she had found in a tiny farming village turned refuge for the masses. She tried to decide which one pulled at her more. When her head touched the pillow that night and her eyes finally closed, she still hadn't figured that out.

CHAPTER SEVENTEEN

Julianne regarded the huddled villagers in front of her.

"We're going to move as fast as we can," she explained. "You'll be able to rest once we reach the next town. Anrock is a day and a half's ride away if we go at a reasonable pace."

"We'll have to spend the night on the road?" a timid voice called.

She nodded. "Yes, but we'll keep you safe. We've had experience fighting the remnant, both the normal hordes and those bound to Skrima. You've seen us fight, though. You know we can handle it." Julianne injected a note of cheerful confidence into her voice.

Jackson waved a hand to get her attention. "You keep saying that word 'Skrima.' What does that mean?"

Julianne took a breath and blew it out slowly. These people had been through a lot, and they were about to face a difficult trip; she didn't want to scare them. However, they needed to know what they might be up against.

"All across Irth, rifts have been opening; portals that lead to other worlds. Skrima are the red beasts that come through. There are several types: some small, some enormous, and some even seem to be friendly."

She waited, running her eyes over the small crowd as her words sank in. One bonus of her audience being so terrified they could barely breathe was that there really wasn't room for greater fear. They seemed to take it in stride. "The remnant we fought today had Skrima attached to their brain stems. The Skrima were controlling the remnant."

"The wee beasties make the remnant faster, but that don't mean we can't smash 'em on their heads," Garrett said confidently. "Ye just have ta be quick on yer feet. Aim fer the head and *smack*!" Garrett smacked his hands together, and his display made more than one person flinch.

"Thank you, Garrett," Julianne said, her voice flat.

Garrett grinned. "Yer welcome!"

"The rules once we're on the road are simple," Marcus said, stepping forward. "Stay together, keep up, and make sure you speak up if there's a problem. We would rather stop as a team and deal with anything that comes up than have somebody lag behind and we have to circle back." He too ran his eyes over the crowd, stopping to look each person in the eye. "We leave no one behind, you hear me? *No one.*"

Marcus's words seemed to inject some confidence in those watching. Julianne felt the blanket of fear lift just a bit, and their audience stood a little taller.

"Are we ready?" she called.

Heads nodded, and she heard a few grumbled cries of "yes" and "will do." Not the rousing agreement she'd hoped for, but it would have to suffice for now.

Jackson stepped out from amongst his people and turned to face them. "We owe these people more than our lives. We owe them our *pride*. They came back after we sent them away and offered their lives for ours. We owe it to them to do as they ask and to take this chance they're giving us."

He turned to Julianne, though he continued to address his audience. "After all this is over we may even be able to come back. We'll return to our little village and rebuild. We'll paint our houses, play in the streets, work the fields, and remember what it's like to live. I for one am done hiding in fear, and it's thanks to these people."

There was a smatter of applause and Julianne smiled. Though she could have gotten the same reaction through magic, the platitudes would have meant nothing. To see it happen organically lifted her spirits like nothing else could have.

"Okay, people, let's go!" Marcus called, waving his arm to direct them along the path to Anrock. The crowd moved out, shuffling at first but picking up speed when they reached the open road.

Julianne pulled herself up on her horse and nudged it over to ride beside Polly near the head of the group.

"How's the leg?" she asked.

Polly shrugged. "I don't think it's as bad as I thought it was, since I can move my foot now. I just hope I don't end up with some revolting disease from the remnant's slimy teeth." She shuddered at the idea.

"Polly, you said you didn't kill the remnant you fought. Tell me again what happened." Julianne listened intently as Polly told her about the remnant who had run into the forest after Polly killed the Skrim that had controlled it.

"It wasn't like looking into the eyes of a remnant," Polly finished. "I could swear it understood. Like there was a mind behind the crazy."

Julianne nodded absentmindedly, her attention soon fading from the girl beside her as she embraced her magic. Her eyes glowed as she channeled a spell through the glittering bracelet on her wrist.

Margit, I want you to find everything we have on the remnant.

The what? Margit's voice was laced with irritation and she sounded distracted.

I think the Skrima are somehow affecting the remnant. I want to know if it can be replicated, and most of all I want to know if it's something that can give us an edge against these alien assholes.

Margit transmitted a mental sigh. *Oh, all right. I'll put one of the initiates to work in the records room.* Margit paused when her attention was diverted.

Julianne waited for a moment, then gently prodded the old woman again. *Are you busy? If you are I can go.*

Busy? Of course I'm bloody busy. I'm doing your job, remember?

Julianne allowed her mirth to pass through their bond. *And you know how much I appreciate that, don't you?*

Enough to rush back to the Heights and relieve me of it? Margit asked eagerly.

Julianne chuckled out loud when she heard that. Despite the old woman's complaints, she sensed the renewed sense of purpose that Margit felt and her enjoyment at the challenge she had been set.

I'm tempted to leave you in charge permanently, Julianne sent, then followed it with a burst of laughter. *Don't worry, I wouldn't really do that to you. It's just that you seem to be enjoying the clerical side of things much more than I do.*

A burst of mock horror flooded the transmission, quickly followed by a resigned sigh. *I am quite good at it, aren't I?*

You are. Having you there to look after that side of things leaves me free to travel the countryside, Julianne replied.

You don't want to come back, do you? Margit asked dryly.

It's not that I don't want to come back, Julianne explained. *But I'm really enjoying my freedom. If there's a chance I can keep traveling, I'll take it. Oh, Margit, the places that I have seen. The people on this side of the Madlands are so different from those in Arcadia and the Heights.*

Well, you stay out there and have your fun for as long as you need to, Margit told her. *I've got things in hand here, and although we miss you, we seem to be getting along okay without you.*

Julianne did her best to send Margit every ounce of the gratitude that suffused her. Hearing the old woman's words was like a balm to her heart. It eased Julianne's anxiety about leaving the Heights again so soon after returning and staying away for so long now.

Though she knew she would have left the Heights even without Margit's assistance, Julianne felt privileged to have such a capable, kind woman looking after things while she was away.

Thank you, Margit.

You're welcome, Margit replied primly. *If I come up with any new information I'll be sure to send it along straight away.*

"Who were you talking to?" Polly asked, bringing Julianne back.

Julianne jumped. She had almost forgotten she had a companion.

"One of the mystics on the Heights," she explained. "I asked her to track down information about the remnant, though I don't think there's anything back there we don't already know."

Polly looked at her skeptically. "So, you don't think I'm crazy?"

Julianne grinned. "I know you're not. I can tell, remember?"

Relief spread across Polly's face and she returned her attention to her horse.

The steady clop of hooves approached and Julianne looked back to see Garrett heading toward them. He rode past the long line of travelers with a deep scowl on his face.

"Garrett, you look miserable!" Polly called.

His scowl deepened and he gestured for her to be quiet.

"Keep yer voice down. Ye don't want ta be scarin' the locals," he warned her in a low voice once he was closer.

"You're worried," Julianne guessed.

Garrett nodded. "We're travelin' wi' an awful lot of people.

This group is a big fat target. How're we goin' ta keep everyone together if we're attacked?"

"You think our biggest problem will be people running off?" Julianne asked.

Garrett nodded again. "When people are afraid they do stupid shit like runnin' off inta the bushes alone where they'll be eaten by hungry bears. Or remnant. Or tigers, wolves, lice—"

"We get the picture." Julianne laughed. "I can't do much about the lice, but I can stop people from running away."

Her eyes glowed white as she sought the other mystic, who was riding at the very back of the procession. *Danil, you need to listen to this,* she sent. A moment later she felt his presence in her mind, watching through her eyes and using her ears to listen.

"If ye use yer magic ta keep everyone in one place it'll be much easier for us ta keep 'em safe," Garrett said. "Though it might make the lice problem even worse."

Lice problem? What lice problem? Danil sent in alarm.

Never mind that. Garrett is worried that if something attacks, people will try to run off. He has a good point. If something happens, I'll need you to work with me on this.

Sure, Danil sent. *Shouldn't be too hard. This lot aren't exactly known for their mental fortitude.*

You might be surprised, Julianne sent.

He thought of Annabeth and her bravery in the face of the earlier attack. *You might just be right there.*

How is she doing? Julianne asked gently.

Danil sent her a view of the young woman riding a short way ahead of him. She was riding one of the few horses that had been left in the town and clutched the saddle horn warily. She was exhausted, but still had a set to her shoulders that suggested she wouldn't be giving up anytime soon.

She is in pain, but dealing with it surprisingly well, Danil sent. *I eased it as much as I could, but unless she finds a druid...* His thoughts trailed off, since he was unwilling to go so far as to blatantly point out that her face would be ruined.

You might care more about that than she does, Julianne said gently. *Annabeth is no flighty young girl. She is smart enough to value a quick mind and a steady hand over good looks...just like you do*, she added pointedly. Julianne felt the heat rise in Danil's face and dropped the subject, satisfied she had made her point.

Oh, she knew Danil would be just as in love with Polly if she wasn't a tiny thing with a beautiful face. Polly's take-no-prisoners attitude, smart mouth, and strong personality were what had drawn Danil to her, even if the man hadn't known it. Still, it didn't hurt to remind him of that every so often

"If ye can bunch the people up in the middle," Garrett said, oblivious to the fact Julianne's attention had shifted, "we can have one group fightin' from the front and one group at the back. That is, if we're surrounded. But even if an attack only comes from one end, we need to make sure we've got someone watchin' at the other."

Julianne nodded. "Good point. If Danil and I are at opposite ends at all time we will be able to communicate instantly. Our fighters can go where they're needed, but Danil and I best stay separated for now."

Garrett nodded in agreement. He had lost the ferocious scowl, which Julianne pointed out.

"A man can't relax unless he has a good plan ta follow," Garrett said. "Even if he hopes he doesn't have ta use it...luck be willin'."

"I think our luck has run out," Julianne murmured quietly. Her eyes glowed as she stretched her magic out farther. "There's a mass of static up ahead, and they're moving toward us." She stood in her stirrups and shaded her eyes with a hand, but the tightly-intertwined foliage of the forest and a tight bend in the mountainous road meant she couldn't see more than a few hundred meters ahead.

"Static? Garrett asked. "Is that remnant or the red beasties?"

"Remnant, I think," Julianne told him. "Be on your guard."

Garrett nodded, and Julianne passed the message to Danil and Marcus. She told the other mystic to stay where he was in case of an attack from their rear.

I'll give our new friends a bit of a nudge, Julianne sent to Danil. *I may need you to maintain it once we're fighting, though.* She muttered a spell that allowed her to make a rather potent suggestion to the people with them.

Stay together. Don't run. Running is dangerous. There is safety in numbers. You are safer together. She repeated the words like a mantra, sinking deeply into the psyche of each person from Kells.

Although they didn't notice the magic being used on them, the villagers clumped into a bunch as far from the edges of the road as possible. Instead of eyes darting toward the false safety of the dense growth lining the roads the people turned inward, taking refuge and comfort in each other.

Even little Flea was firmly caught by the spell, burying herself among the people around her. Julianne breathed a sigh of relief glad the girl's magic hadn't also given her a strong blocking ability.

I can take it from here, Danil sent. When she felt him take over the spell Julianne let go. The handover was seamless and allowed Julianne to focus her attention on the horde of enemies headed their way.

And what a horde it is. The buzz swelled inside her mind and she tried to guess the numbers they faced. Upward of twenty, maybe more.

CHAPTER EIGHTEEN

Garrett gripped the haft of his axe tightly, adjusting his grip to compensate for the thin sheen of sweat that covered his hands.

It was rare for him to feel nervous before a battle, but knowing they only had five points of defense over such a large area—one packed with so many people—gave him the heebie-jeebies. It wasn't that he doubted he could take down whatever army approached. It was doing it without innocent casualties that gave him pause.

They're coming closer, Julianne sent. Garrett shivered both at the impending battle and the uncomfortable feeling of someone being inside his head.

He had taken point, placing himself at the front of their small formation. Marcus stood to his left, Julianne was to his right, and Polly was behind him to catch any remnant that might slip through. Danil had taken the rear, keeping watch in case another attack sprang from behind.

Despite Garrett's distrust of magic in general and his loathing of it being used on him, he appreciated that it *could* be useful.

When Garrett crouched he felt the slightest tremble through

the soles of his boots, so he pressed two fingers to the ground. "Here they come!"

He pulled his axe in closer, angled it to one side, and pointed it slightly toward the sky. Anyone could clearly see he was prepared to fight.

The trail ahead darkened, then screaming monsters exploded from the trees. The remnant horde filled the road, jostling each other as they ran. Garrett gripped his axe tighter.

They came nearer, and he blew out a slow breath. If anyone had told him his method for preparing for battle closely resembled a mystic embracing a trance he'd have laughed. He reached for the part of himself that was quiet and focused; the part that reacted on instinct rather than thought. The part that was engineered to protect and defend.

The horde raced closer. Garrett sucked in a breath and prepared to dive forward.

The enemy group split like a parting wave, a synchronized move that sent the horde past Garrett, Marcus, and Julianne and out of the reach of their weapons. Their eyes were focused ahead rather than on the tempting mass of victims huddled in the center of the road

Garrett's jaw dropped in shock, and a moment later he yelped when he realized that the first ranks of the remnant army had already passed him.

Garrett spun, expecting to see carnage behind him.

Instead he saw the teaming mass racing down the road, leaving an empty path on either side of the refugees.

"What the fuck are they doin'?" Garrett yelled.

Julianne raised a hand to hush him and called, "I don't know, but let's not start a fight if we don't need to."

Garrett's rough headcount suggested that might be the prudent option. At least a hundred remnant had hurtled past, far too many for the fighters to defeat while guaranteeing the safety of their charges.

The ground shook under the weight of the remnant's rotten boots hitting the ground in perfect unison. The air was filled with incoherent babble, the whimpers of terrified people, and the occasional squeal of fright. Soon, though, the only sound remaining was the panicked panting of the villagers left behind.

Garrett shook his head in wonder. "What were they thinkin'? None of 'em attacked. Were they scared?" His shoulders straightened. "I mean, I know I'm gettin' meself a bit of a reputation, but really!"

He chose to ignore Julianne's eye-roll. "You certainly do have a...*reputation*, but I don't think that caused this. It almost looked like they were on a mission. Perhaps in search of Skrima?"

Garrett shook his head. "Whatever it was, it's one fer the books. I've never seen anythin' like that in me life."

"You're telling me!" Marcus agreed in a low voice. "Remnant running from a fight?"

"Julianne, what if they *are* after Skrima?" Polly asked. "Is there any risk of running into an even bigger battle if we keep moving?"

"You've got a good point there," Julianne said and she fell silent, eyes lighting up. When they cleared, her shoulders dropped in relief. "I can't sense anything ahead. I want to get moving as fast as possible and leave those guys behind."

"Glad ta have a plan," Garrett said with a grin. "Up ye get. Come on, stop yer lollygaggin' and start walkin'!"

Garrett traipsed through the crowd of confused people and went over to untie his horse from the side of the road. He had secured it there earlier, unwilling to trust the stupid beast in a fight.

"They didn't even stop fer the horses!" Garrett mumbled. "What were they thinkin'?" He eyed the equine. "That's the second time ye've dodged a bullet, horse," he said. "Is there somethin' wrong wi' ye?"

The horse snorted but didn't answer. Shaking his head again

in disbelief, Garrett mounted and gave the horse a solid kick. "Get goin', ye crusty old nag."

"Danil, let's get these people moving," Julianne called, her eyes flashing white a moment before Danil's did. The people milling about turned toward their destination as one, stepping out in the same eerie unison as the horde that had just passed.

A few minutes later Julianne let go of her spell with relief. Shaking off the uneasy sensation brought on by the similarities between the people of Kells and the mindless monsters, she wondered what exactly they would find in Anrock.

They traveled until dusk. When they reached another fork in the road, Julianne only needed a cursory glance at the map to tell they needed to take the western trail.

She sent the instructions ahead to Danil, who now led their entourage. When he didn't immediately respond she reached out again, this time adding a gentle prod.

Danil's response worried her.

I know which way to go, Jules, but unfortunately this damn horse has other ideas. He's flat refusing to listen to me. He keeps shying away from the road every time I pull him to that side.

The hint of worry in Danil's thoughts echoed Julianne's.

"Let's take a short break, shall we?" she called, keeping her voice casual. Garrett shot a questioning glance over his shoulder. When Julianne gave a minute shake of her head, his eyes widened.

"Ye heard what the mystic said. We've got a ways ta go, and we don't want yer sorry asses slowin' us down cuz yer tired. Take a break, and if ye've got somethin' ta eat, eat it now."

Garrett was less effective at disguising the concern in his voice, but no one seemed to notice.

The villagers were worn out from the journey and the fight that had preceded it, not to mention the months of bone-deep fear that had sapped what little energy they'd had.

Garrett wheeled his horse around once he was sure everyone

had come to a halt. Julianne didn't wait for him to approach, but nudged her horse toward the rearick.

"Need me ta go for a wee walk?" he asked in a low voice.

Julianne nodded. "I'll come with you. I don't know what's ahead, but the horses are sensing...something."

Garrett nodded sagely. "The cantankerous bastards have a sense fer trouble. At least," he added as he slapped his mount's neck, "the ones who aren't as dumb as bricks."

Danil, stay here with Polly and Marcus. Julianne sent the instructions not only to the other mystic but to the rest of their party as well. *Garrett and I will go and scout the path ahead. Try not to alarm anyone, but be ready to move if we need to.*

Since she was still touching Marcus' mind, Julianne could feel the protest he was about to launch. She tossed him a glance, rolled her eyes, and shook her head. Marcus slumped in resignation, raised his hands in surrender, and nodded.

"Let's go." Julianne kicked her horse to the front of the group with Garrett close on her tail.

A few moments later she pulled to a halt, noting her mount's anxious snorts. The horse shook his head and tried to turn away from the western trail.

"Maybe we should walk the rest of the way," Julianne suggested.

Garrett, whose horse danced even more nervously than Julianne's, eagerly agreed.

"It's not that I don't like horses," he explained once his feet were solidly on the ground. "It's just that I *really* don't like horses."

"I think the feeling is mutual." Marcus nodded at Garrett's mount, which had skittered as far from the rearick as it could.

Garrett eyeballed the beast and snorted. "Let's get on wi' it."

"Horse! Stay wi' the pretty soldier boy, ye hear? He's got my permission ta turn ye into glue if ye misbehave."

Marcus chuckled and grabbed the indignant beast's reins. "You two be careful out there, ok?"

Julianne let Garrett take the lead as they slowly made their way along the overgrown road. Garrett strained his ears for trouble, but he heard nothing.

"The damn quiet is more unnerving than the sounds of battle," Garrett griped, and Julianne nodded in agreement.

"Not even the birds are whistling," she remarked.

Garrett shivered as goosebumps ran along his skin. Rubbing his arms to flatten the hairs that had bristled, he opened his mouth to speak, then stopped. He put a hand out to warn Julianne.

The rearick cupped a hand to his ear, straining to identify the rasping and sucking noise up ahead. He cursed the serpentine trails, wishing that they were on flat ground with straight roads instead of paths winding around hills and gullies.

Silence fell, and Garrett shot a cautious look at Julianne before creeping forward again. With a few quick hand gestures he motioned her off the path and directed her to keep out of sight.

Julianne nodded and faded into the bushes. Garrett took a dozen steps, then looked back for her. If he hadn't known where to look, he would never have noticed her dusty white robes fluttering between the dense tree trunks that lined the road.

Satisfied that she was not only out of sight but could take care of herself even if she were seen, Garrett plowed ahead.

He didn't have to go far.

The smell reached him first. The choking metallic scent of blood soaked the air, filling his lungs and making his stomach heave. Garrett smothered a cough and pulled his shirt over his nose.

A few more steps, and source of the vile odor became clear.

Remnant everywhere, all of them dead and sporting deep wounds. Guts and limbs were strewn across the road and over the piles of bodies.

Garrett jumped at a rustle nearby, then stooped to examine the glassy-eyed remnant who had made the sound.

"You're not dead?" Garrett murmured in surprise.

The beast's torso had been slit open from sternum to pelvis and glossy ropes spilled out of the wound, leaking shit all over the ground.

The remnant gave a half-hearted whimper, the pain in its voice enough to move even the sardonic rearick. Garrett gave his axe a tiny flick to adjust his grip, then lifted it and brought it down in a single swing. The whimpering stopped.

Garrett glanced around to see if Julianne had witnessed his act of mercy, but she was nowhere to be seen. He shook off the prickling feeling that he was being watched and stomped through the remainder of the battlefield. Apart from the lone survivor they were all dead, each from a gruesome wound and each displaying defensive wounds.

Putting the mass of bodies out of his mind, Garrett focused his attention on the soft dirt of the road and the nearby bushes, but the mess of boot- and footprints was too jumbled for him to discern what had happened.

After following the trail for some distance, he got the impression that the remnant had been traveling as a group before turning on each other for no obvious reason. Even Garrett was unsure how they had dealt such grievous harm to each other without leaving any survivors.

He moved back to the beginning of the trail, squinting closely at the ground.

"Maybe there *were* survivors," he muttered.

"I imagine those who passed us earlier were running from whatever happened here."

Startled by the unexpected voice behind him, Garrett launched himself into the air and let out a shrill squeal.

Julianne laughed. "I didn't mean to scare you."

"Scared?" Garrett grumped, his eyes still scanning for danger. "I ain't scared."

"The question remains," Julianne murmured, looking at the bloodied mess. "Were the Skrima the attackers here or the attacked?"

"Skrima?" Garrett squinted at the mystic, wondering what her magic had revealed.

Noticing his bewilderment, Julianne pointed at something half-obscured by a limp body—the crushed shell of one of the smaller Skrima they had seen in this region. Garrett scanned the ground and quickly found more evidence of the small beasts.

Julianne turned the remnant's body over with her boot to look at the back of its head and nudged the base of the remnant's skull with her toe.

"Oh." Garrett squatted next to the corpse and leaned closer to examine the bloody hole. He thrust a finger at some marks— three scratches surrounding the wound, pointing toward the center. "Is that how the little bastards latch on?"

"I imagine so," Julianne said. "But what's that?"

Julianne pointed one end of her staff at the hole in the remnant's neck. Just as Garrett was about to explain to her it was a hole in a head, he realized what she was pointing at.

Under the matted hair, swollen flesh, and streaks of congealed blood, something was almost hidden. Though a red lump on the side of someone's head would not normally be anything to remark upon, this one looked different.

Garrett grabbed a dagger from his boot and dug into the lump. He slipped the knife in a little deeper, twisted it just the right way, and flicked it out. A long white wormlike thread stretched from the tip of the knife back to the remnant's head.

As he pulled the blade away the appendage stretched and then snapped off with a wet pop, flying off the knife and landing in the dirt several feet away. It twitched and thrashed for a moment before spasming into a tight knot and falling still.

This time Julianne didn't comment on Garrett's squeal—possibly because she had let one out herself.

"That. Is. Disgusting!" Julianne said, injecting more feeling into the phrase than she ever had in her life.

Garrett nodded, eyes wide. "That's putting it nicely. What is it?"

"It's part of the Skri—" Julianne began.

"No, no. I know that. But is that how they control the remnant?" Garrett prodded the wormlike length with the tip of his knife, but it had hardened and didn't react. "What would happen if ye stuck one o' those in me brain?"

Julianne shuddered with the implications of his question. "Nothing good, I would imagine. Let's hope we never have to find out."

Garrett stood and shook his head. "Well, no matter what happened here, we've got a whole bunch of people back there ta deal with. We can't let 'em see this. They'll shit their pants and run for the hills, magic spell be damned. Do ye think ye can fuck wi' their minds enough that they don't see it?"

Julianne considered it. "I can't guarantee it. If anything goes wrong, the illusion might slip. And getting them past without at least one falling onto one of these bodies would be almost impossible."

"Is there a way around?" Garrett asked.

Julianne frowned, her mind going back over the map she had left on her horse. "I think so. We'll take the other trail. I think it joins up with this one farther down. I'd rather lose a day of travel than subject our new friends to a sight like this."

CHAPTER NINETEEN

Julianne sat by her tent, watching the low hum of activity on the other side of the campfire. Beside her, Danil flipped a bronze coin over the backs of his fingers.

"How can we keep all of these people safe," Julianne whispered, "when it feels like the whole world wants us all dead?"

Danil shrugged. "We can't. Not all of them, at any rate, and not forever. Even the ones we protect from aliens and remnant will eventually die of old age, or illness, or childbirth. Or maybe tumble off a cliff that drunk rearick—"

"You're not helping," Julianne said dryly.

"Sorry, but I stand by my point. You *can't* keep everyone safe. It's not your job." Julianne began to protest, but Danil waved her down. "Hear me out. You're the leader of the temple, and that's a job that you do very well. I know you *feel* like it's your job to protect the whole world from harm, it's not. Oh, it's your job to *try*—but that's also my job, and Marcus's, and Garrett's, and everyone else's. It's the responsibility of all humanity to do our best to keep each other safe. And even though it's our job to try, that doesn't mean we'll succeed. And even if we don't succeed, it doesn't mean we failed."

Julianne rubbed her head, watching the ever-moving coin glitter in the firelight. "I'm sure you had a point in there somewhere, Danil, but if you did I missed it."

Danil sighed. "If you saw a woman standing on the side of the road with no home and no money and no help and she had a horrible disease, you would feel compelled to help her, right?"

"Yes," Julianne said dubiously, wondering where his train of thought was leading.

"You'd give her some money, find her a doctor, and make sure she found a place to stay." Danil flipped the coin at Julianne and she caught it. "But that doesn't make it your job to heal every illness that ever existed, does it? Or to spend the rest of your life going from city to city to make sure every single person has a home?"

Julianne's brows knitted together as she contemplated his words, but after a minute she slowly nodded. "It's my job to defeat the monsters in front of me and to try my best to save the people that I can...and as long as I'm doing my best to save them, I'm fulfilling my duty. Is that what you're saying?"

Danil grinned happily. "And may I say that you're doing a damn fine job of it?"

Still dissatisfied with her inability to rid the world of remnant, Julianne slumped. Danil leaned closer and slipped an arm around her shoulders. "Cheer up, Jules. I know it's hard, but you need to remember... There are *so* many people alive today because of you; so many people safe and happy back in Tahn and Muir. Not to mention the people you helped back in Arcadia."

Polly sauntered over and sat down on Julianne's other side. "What's got you down?" she asked gently.

"She's pissed that bad stuff happens and sad that she can't stop it all," Danil explained.

"Then let's change that. Tomorrow we'll march out and punch the bad stuff in the face. Really fuck it up, maybe knock a few teeth out. Yeah?" Polly slipped her arm through Julianne's and beamed a smile at the mystic. "I mean, look at all the bad guys we've kicked in the teeth just in the last couple of months. I'm sure we can handle a few more!"

That brought a smile to Julianne's lips. "You're damn right."

By morning Julianne's spirits had lifted. The sun dawned bright and clear, and despite the flies that had come with summer's warmth, she rolled out of bed feeling a sliver of hope.

Danil's words had helped, and so had Polly's. Maybe she couldn't save *everyone*—but she would damn well try, and she wouldn't go down without one hell of a fight. Not only that, she had her friends beside her every step of the way.

The camp was already beginning to mobilize. Everyone was on their feet, shoving blankets into bags, chewing on old bread, or milling about the edges of the group. All were eager to get moving on the last day of their journey toward Anrock and safety.

Julianne pulled the map out, wincing at the smudges and creases that covered it. "Now that we're back on the main road, we should be able to reach Anrock in half a day."

"Anrock?" a voice behind her asked. Julianne turned to see Tilda, a woman from Kells, behind her. "You're not taking us *there*, are you?"

"Yes," Julianne said carefully. "Is there a reason we shouldn't?"

Tilda snorted. "You can take us there, but they won't let us in. Everyone knows Anrock is closed to outsiders."

Julianne narrowed her eyes. Her opinion of the town's leader was already low, thanks to rumors she had heard back in Tahn. "You mean they wouldn't even let in refugees?" she asked in an edgy voice.

"Not a chance." Tilda laughed. "That bastard Coates wouldn't even let his own mother in if she was stupid enough to set foot outside the town walls."

"What?" Julianne asked in shock. "Why?"

"Bastard takes it as a personal affront if anyone leaves, no matter that they've got no food or supplies and no room left behind those tall stone walls." Tilda shrugged. "Well, they might have a little more room now. Last *I* heard, a bunch of people left to start a settlement of their own. Haven't heard back from them, though."

Julianne wondered if the group she referred to was Patrick's or if more people had tried to leave. Shaking off the stray thought, Julianne set her shoulders. "We're going to Anrock and we *will* be welcomed there if it's the last thing I do."

The exhausted group made it to Anrock unscathed under the dusky tones of twilight, and Julianne pushed them on until they were directly under its heavily-fortified walls.

Julianne approached the barricaded gates and looked for a brass ring or pull rope to signal their arrival, but found nothing. Frowning, she wondered if this was a deliberate tactic. She rapped loudly on the thick oaken doors.

Nobody answered. Julianne knocked again, though she knew they had been heard; her magic wasn't fooled. The two men on the other side of the gate were doing their best to pretend they hadn't noticed her brisk knock.

Julianne could tell their reluctance was born of fear rather than an aversion to helping innocent people who might be caught outside unprotected. The men quivered, logic saying remnant didn't knock but paranoia insisting it was a subterfuge to let the monsters in to ravage the town.

"Hello? My name is Julianne. Please open the door."

Biting her lip, Julianne considered whether a mental nudge would be required. Despite her earlier refusal to use magic, she understood that in this case she might be well justified in tweaking some emotions to keep the terrified people of Kells out of harm's way.

Danil remarked quietly from beside her, "You know, they've cleared a significant area around the town. If we camp here overnight we should be safe. As long as we've got someone on guard, we'll see anything coming with plenty of time to react."

"Danil, what the hell kind of remnant would introduce themselves by name and use manners to request entry?" she asked, still distracted by the mental gymnastics of the men who barred their entry to Anrock.

They were picturing a horde at the gates, one with the intelligence to use such tricks to gain entry to the fortified stronghold.

"Everything sounds scarier in the dark," Danil reminded her. "We know we can force our way in if we need to, but why push it?"

Julianne eyed the sky, which was speckled with stars from one horizon to the other. There wasn't a single cloud in sight, and Danil was right—the city walls were in the middle of the clearing. It would be enough to give them a degree of safety. Julianne's eyes glowed again and she quickly touched on the minds of the men inside to confirm that they would be on guard until morning. They also lacked any mental barriers that might prevent her from forcing them to open the gates in an emergency.

Julianne turned to the sea of crestfallen faces that had followed her from their tiny, unprotected town.

"It seems Anrock is closed for the night," Julianne said calmly. "We will be safe outside until dawn."

"What if they don't let us in in the morning?" Jackson asked. "Will we have to turn around and go back?"

"The leader of this city has a responsibility to provide refuge if at all possible." Julianne placed her hands on her hips, her expression growing dark. "Bitch help him if he decides to shirk that responsibility."

Her emotional words seemed to instill hope in those around her. Anxiety faded as one by one her audience turned away to begin the task of setting up camp for the night.

"So," Marcus began as he sauntered over. "How are those ethics of yours going?"

Julianne scowled. "Are you questioning my judgment?"

Marcus shook his head. "I think you're doing the right thing. I always do. And I know you're prepared to follow through with that threat. I just hope you're prepared to deal with the fallout."

"What fallout?" Julianne asked, a seed of doubt sprouting.

Marcus's gaze softened. "Most of the time, the thing you *have* to do is the thing you *want* to do. When the thing you have to do is something you're trying to avoid... Well, I know how much that eats you up."

Julianne sighed and dropped her shoulders. "You're right. I'd really like to get out of this without having to warp anybody's mind or having to force people to do the right thing, but in this case I don't think that's going to happen."

"What did ye see when yer eyes were glowin'?" Garrett asked. "Are they plannin' ta feed us ta the wolves?"

"No, that's just it." Julianne glanced around to make sure no one else was close enough to overhear. "The men at the gates *wanted* to open it. Or at least, a part of them did, but their minds were so clouded with fear they couldn't see reason."

"Whaddaya mean?" Garret asked.

"They heard me knocking," Julianne explained, "but they were terrified. Of remnant, of Skrima; even of their leader. Even though the logical part of their minds was screaming that it was fine, that we were just people, they couldn't get past that fear."

"So they left us to die," Marcus spat, resting his hands on his hips as his mouth twisted with disgust. "Knowing we're out here as remnant bait."

Julianne shook her head. "Their minds are so torn up it's created cognitive dissonance. They're scared of what we might be, and equally scared of what might happen to *us* if they let us in. They actually managed to convince themselves that the sound of my fist bashing on their gate was just the wind."

"That's some pretty serious self-delusion," Danil commented.

"Do you think this Coates guy has been scaring them with false stories? Has he made threats about people coming inside?"

Julianne shrugged. "The guards weren't really thinking of specifics, and I didn't want to push. Not just yet, anyway. If morning comes and they still won't let us in, we will find out more."

"I'll take first watch," Garrett said. "Polly can take the second, and Marcus the third. That way ye and yer glowy-eyed bastard of a friend can get a good night's sleep. I think yer goin' ta need it." Garrett gave a nod to indicate his decision was final and stomped off to tell Polly the good news.

"Glowy-eyed bastard?" Danil said, a grin pulling at the corners of his lips. "That's the nicest thing he's said to me all week!"

"I do believe you're right," Julianne said. "But if you're willing to forego some of that beauty sleep that was just offered, how about we go do some reconnaissance?"

A grin lit Danil's face. "I'm always down for some subterfuge. Just point me in the right direction."

Julianne sent Marcus a flurry of thoughts, explaining that she and Danil were going to go for a short walk. She didn't want the others to notice her absence. Pulling Danil away from the crowded camp, Julianne led the way around Anrock's walls, one hand trailing on the smooth stone that separated the city from the rest of the world.

They walked together in silence, breathing quietly, then slowed, eyes flaring like bright stars in the deepening night. Julianne felt Danil's magic beside hers as they each sent a tendril of magic into the town to reach nearby minds and scan them for information.

Coates is dead? Danil sent to Julianne, startled.

She nodded, having confirmed the information from a second person. *This wife of his, the one that has taken his place as the town leader...* Julianne's thoughts trailed off as she touched the next mind and resumed once she had released it after finding nothing new. *There's something odd about this situation, Danil. I think we did the right thing by waiting until morning. I don't want to go in there blind.*

I don't exactly get a choice there, Jules, Danil sent, tone light if a little snarky.

Julianne rolled her eyes. *You know what I mean. I want to be as prepared as possible before meeting this woman.*

I can sense their fear, Danil commented. *But that's not unusual, given what's gone on in this neck of the woods lately. What's bothering you?*

That's exactly it, Julianne said sent. *Danil, I just read half a dozen minds and they're all just scared. There's no anger, no grief...just gut-twisting anxiety, vague fears of the remnant, yes, and the Skrima—but also of the dark. They're afraid—they're all afraid—of being alone and of...*

Bees? Danil's eyes met Julianne's, confusion etched on his features even in the moonlight. *Why would everyone be afraid of bees? I don't see an event that caused this...*

Narrowing his eyes, Danil reached out to another person. The mind he brushed was that of a young woman, and he felt the rush of flavor as soup touched her tongue.

Tammy sat at the table with her husband, gently sipping the soup she had just prepared. The bland taste barely registered in the woman's mind as her heart raced with unsettling discomfort.

Tammy briefly wondered if she were about to have a heart attack, then considered that might be for the best. It wasn't like she was happy, and she guessed that dying that way would be infinitely better than being torn to shreds by one of those monsters outside. Her heart thumped even harder at that thought.

Yes, perhaps it would be easier this way, she thought idly as she took another mouthful of soup, swallowing hard to force it past the lump in her throat.

Danil carefully withdrew, slipping into the head of Tammy's husband.

Gordon absently noted that his wife was wearing the same dress she had worn yesterday, and her face was still marked by a smudge from when she had cleaned the fireplace earlier that morning.

It's shaped like a bird, Gordon thought, the idea quickly consuming his mind. *Perhaps it's a sign...a sign of the end. We're doomed. The remnant, the monsters, the bees... We're cursed, just like Catherine told us.*

Danil teased that tiny thread of information, delicately pulling it out to examine it.

Catherine, the young, frightened girl who stood next to Coates on his wedding day, looked more like a terrified child than a beautiful bride. Strangely, her anxiety was mirrored by a pit of worry in Gordon's gut. Later the same girl, pale and drawn at her husband's funeral, shivered into her thick furs as Gordon watched with the other townspeople, whispering about curses and warnings of doom.

Gordon shifted uncomfortably in his chair and put down his spoon, appetite suddenly gone.

Dammit, Danil thought. *I wasn't careful enough.*

He let the vague thought float back into Gordon's subconscious.

Something—or someone—is fucking with this guy's feelings, Danil said to Julianne.

She nodded grimly. *Not just him. It's like the whole town is suffocating under a blanket of terror. On the surface the city looks peaceful and well run, but living like this? Danil, this isn't living.*

Do we think Catherine is behind this? Danil asked carefully.

Julianne hesitated and bit her lip. As much as she wanted to blame the strange woman who seemed to have taken over the town, there wasn't enough evidence yet—and Julianne was aware that she was biased. The memories of Donna's role in Rogan's cult were still fresh in her memory, as raw as the day Julianne had killed her.

"Let's go back," Julianne said quietly. "Polly will be missing you, and if our new friends notice we have been gone for any length of time they may start to worry."

Danil nodded pensively and turned on his heel to walk back.

They had only been gone for ten minutes, but in that time the campsite had been organized. Polly strode over holding a stack of blankets and bedrolls, smoke slowly winding into the air behind her as two men leaned over a small firepit.

"Did you find anything?" Polly asked quietly. She darted a glance over her shoulder to make sure no one had followed her.

"When morning comes I'll go in alone," Julianne told them.

"You've got to be kidding me!" Danil exclaimed. "Alone? You admitted you don't know what you're up against!"

Julianne shrugged. "If I can't take care of this alone, you're better off losing only me. I don't want these people left unprotected. I don't think smuggling them into a hostile city and leaving them to fend for themselves while I hunt down Catherine is going to do anyone any favors."

"Let Danil and me go," Polly said. She glanced from one mystic to the other, completely ignorant of the threat that lay inside but willing to go up against it regardless. "From what little you've said it sounds like some mindfuckery will be needed in there. Danil can take care of that while I act as his eyes—and his blade."

"You know I love it when you talk tough," Danil said, leaning toward her for a kiss. Polly rolled her eyes and stepped back, causing him to stumble and almost fall on the dirt.

"That might not be such a bad idea," Julianne mused. "But what if you fall under some kind of mystic spell? Danil won't be able to fight our enemy and keep you safe too."

Polly shrugged. "We both know that sometimes sacrifices

have to be made. I have no doubt that Danil would make the right decision."

Danil paled. "I'm glad *you're* confident. Because I can't see myself leaving you in danger while I save the world."

"She's right," Julianne said. "I've known you long enough to know you'll do the right thing."

Danil didn't look convinced but he didn't argue.

"Right," Julianne said. "It's settled then. At dawn, you two make your way into the city. Stay in contact the whole time." Julianne jangled her bracelet to remind him that distance no longer created a barrier to their communication.

"I suppose if this goes well Polly will get all the credit, and if we fuck up it'll be my fault." Danil heaved a sigh.

Polly clapped him on the shoulder. "You're learning! I knew my lessons were starting to sink in."

Danil couldn't smother the chuckle that bubbled out. "You're such a smartass."

"You two go and get some sleep. You'll need to be alert and ready for action tomorrow," Julianne said.

Polly and Danil nodded and made their way to the meager supply of rations. Julianne watched as Danil quickly counted the small parcels that were left, mostly loaves of bread and strips of dried meat carefully packaged in oiled cloth. She pursed her lips when both turned without taking anything for themselves.

She would have done the same. There had been so little food left in Kells when they had arrived that they hadn't been able to adequately supply for the journey.

Using a thin sliver of mental magic to quell the grumbling of her stomach, Julianne wandered off to find Marcus. She intended to crawl into her bedroll once she had informed him of their plan and sleep until dawn. She had no doubt there would be no rest after that until this spell suffocating Anrock had been lifted and everyone was safe inside the fortified walls.

CHAPTER TWENTY

Julianne sat quietly in the back of Danil's mind as he patiently waited for someone to respond to his obnoxiously loud calls.

"Come out, come out, wherever you are!" Danil called again, hands cupped to his mouth, but the doors stayed closed. Danil threw a glance at Julianne and shrugged, and in the early morning sun she saw his eyes light up.

Danil reached out to the gatekeeper to give him a mental command. It wasn't difficult; although the man had initially refused to open the gate, he had been conflicted. The gatekeeper knew what lurked outside, and his instinct was to protect the people who turned up asking for refuge. It was only his deep-seated fear of what lurked outside that had stopped him from removing the heavy barricade. *Queen Catherine warned us of the monsters in the forest, but... Oh, Bitch, what if they end up cursed like us?*

Queen? Danil sent to Julianne. *Curse?*

She didn't respond, but Danil felt her note the strange references. Once he had given the gatekeeper a hard-enough prod, the gates scraped and creaked as they were opened. Gripping Polly's hand tightly, the couple stepped inside.

"I'll let *you* in," the man said, throwing a nervous glance beyond the mystic. "Just you two. Two is bad enough. I can't be letting a whole country full of strangers inside, not when the risks are... Well, you understand, don't you?"

The man looked at Danil, pleading for the mystic to accept his decision. Taking pity on the man due to the great strain he was under, Danil nodded. "You can close that again. I'm sure that once we speak to Catherine you'll know what to do next."

A cloud of confusion passed over the man's face, but he quickly turned back to swing the tall and heavy doors closed. He turned the wheel that lowered the massive beam into place while his companion worked an intricate pulley system to guide it.

"Now we just have to find our benevolent host." Danil straightened and cocked his head to one side as if listening.

"And how are we supposed to do that?" Polly asked, nervously eyeing the neatly cobbled streets. They were still in the shadow of the great wall, and she shivered as a cool breeze dawdled past. A couple of windows were already open, though lanterns still dotted the streets from the previous night.

"Perhaps we should find a guide," Danil suggested.

Polly raised an eyebrow but didn't comment when a middle-aged woman ducked out of her house and hurried over to them. She angled a worried glance at the sky, then dropped her eyes to the ground.

"Hello," the woman said. "Hogan said you needed someone to take you to Catherine. Damned if I know how he even knew you were here... Well, my name is Teagan. Just follow me and we'll have you there in no time."

Teagan self-consciously wiped her hands on her apron, puffs of flour clouding the air as she dusted them off. She trotted down the street with the quick jerky movements of someone headed toward their doom.

"You're not hurting her, are you?" Polly muttered. "I've never actually seen you do this before. Kind of creepy."

"Do what?" Danil asked. "She's not under a spell. Her husband was when he ordered her out here, but Teagan isn't affected by anything."

"Ah, I see." Polly shuddered. "But it's still creepy."

"Hey, I have never hidden what I am," Danil said. He wished he could see her expression, but the nearby townspeople were hiding behind doors and curtains and Teagan had her back to them.

"I never said it was a bad thing," Polly remarked. "It's just weird to watch you do it. I know you'd never use your magic to hurt anyone."

"Well, I certainly *hope* you know that."

Polly darted a glance at the woman ahead. "She can't hear us, can she?" Polly cursed to herself, only now realizing how loudly they'd been talking. Still, Teagan hadn't given any sign she'd over-heard their conversation.

Danil frowned. "She heard everything. She's too scared to say anything, though."

Polly squirmed uneasily. "You weren't kidding when you said this town was weird."

They were taken to a large stone manor toward the center of the city. The building was garish, painted crisp white and deep purple with flashes of red. Through the tall windows that lined the front walls, Danil could see plush green curtains embroidered with lavender flowers. None of the colors quite matched, and the withered brown plants by the front door did nothing to pull the decor together.

Teagan walked up to the door and Polly saw her hand tremble as she lifted it to knock. Danil's eyes were already white since he'd used Polly's sight to navigate the narrow streets, but she heard him mutter something under his breath.

"She's nervous. Not exactly scared of Catherine, but not thrilled to be here either," Danil whispered. Despite Teagan's resolute dismissal of their earlier conversation, he wasn't sure

AMY HOPKINS & MICHAEL ANDERLE

how the woman would react to being spoken about so openly.

Teagan's mouth thinned as she turned to the couple. "There you go. You…uhh…don't want *me* to come in, do you?"

Danil glanced at Polly and raised an eyebrow.

The man who opened the door looked less than pleased at the disturbance. His long narrow face and thick eyebrows were pulled into a sour frown. "Our Queen wishes to know why she is being disturbed," he said, his voice as dour as his expression. "Her nerves are fragile. Surely you know better than to startle her with an unexpected visit?"

Teagan's face fell in dismay, but Danil quickly intervened. With a quickly muttered phrase under his breath, he bowed to the butler. "Queen Catherine has requested our presence. This lovely girl was simply showing us the way. I'm sure Queen Catherine will be just fine."

A brief flicker of confusion crossed the butler's face, then he smiled and bowed to Danil. "Of course, of course. Come this way." He gestured Danil and Polly inside but dropped an arm behind them to prevent Teagan from following. The girl sighed with relief as the door closed in her face.

"Charles, my good man," Danil said with an easy grin, "tell me exactly how young Catherine came to be Queen?"

Charles almost fell over his own feet and a sudden wash of discomfort flooded his face. "I… Um, I don't remember. I'm sure it… It's legitimate, I'm sure it is."

"It's all right. I won't press you for it just yet." Danil spoke flatly, recognizing the signs of a not-so-subtle spell. He dug around in Charles' head, cursing the clumsy spell Catherine had put on him.

Charles shook his head.

"This way." Once the conversation had ceased, Charles sank back into his role as a butler.

Danil wondered exactly what Charles remembered of his

past. He had been a teacher; one with an excellent reputation. He had been in high demand by the city's elite, who wanted only the best tutelage for their children.

He had in fact taught Catherine, though as an adult. She'd requested a tutor after her marriage, and when Coates had died Charles had been absorbed into the household during Catherine's grief.

Charles guided them up the extravagant staircase and down a hallway hung with old tapestries and paintings and finally paused at two ornately carved doors. He gave a single bow before sweeping the doors open.

"Charles! What are you doing? Why are these people in my bedroom?"

Through Danil's connection with Polly, Julianne regarded the girl. Her face still held the softness of youth, despite her sharp cheekbones and pallor. Catherine's eyes were ringed in tired circles and her hands shook as she clutched her shawl tighter.

This girl was probably no more than seventeen, Julianne guessed. Catherine's brown hair hung in limp ringlets above her shoulders, held back from her face by a tarnished bronze tiara.

"Danil?" Polly murmured.

Danil reached out to her, letting Julianne feel the flood of fear that ran through his girlfriend. Both mystics felt Polly wrestle with the emotion as she clenched her hands into fists. She focused on the pain of her nails biting into flesh to distract her from the overwhelming desire to run.

Danil, I don't think this is safe. Julianne sent the warning like a sharp cut. She grew concerned at her fellow mystic's stunned silence. *Danil?*

A pit of worry opened in Julianne's gut. Though mental magic could be incredibly strong, she had *never* seen anything like this. Even Rogan's spells had had intent behind them. Danil's brief look into Catherine's mind, however, showed that this had none. Almost like a child who had grown up speaking to animals and thinking it was the most normal thing in the world, Catherine had no idea that what she was doing had any base in magic.

The girl simply believed that everyone was as afraid as she was. That reinforced her fear, creating a loop that convinced her that if everyone else was scared too her fears must be real.

Julianne sent a sharp mental tug on Danil's mind that jerked him out of his downward spiral into terror and he shook his head, blinked, and cut off his bond with Polly. That seemed to help. With his shields in place—and without the added effect of feeling Polly's distorted emotions—he was able to think a little more clearly.

Bitch's oath, Jules. What the hell do I do about this?

CHAPTER TWENTY-ONE

Catherine regarded the newcomers with a mixture of terror and relief.

"Oh, you poor thing," the man crooned and knelt in front of her. "I'm not here to hurt you. Not at all." His white eyes shone like stars, white-hot. They burned into her soul.

"Please," she gasped. "Take what you want. The jewels are in the dresser over there!" She thrust a jerky hand toward the nearby bureau.

"Sshhhh." The man muttered a word…magic, perhaps? She'd heard of magic, but never seen it. A fireball, she was sure. She braced herself for death.

Warmth spread through her, but not the searing heat of the magical fire. Catherine's heart beat painfully and slowly. Her breath smoothed from ragged gasps into a deep nourishing rhythm that made her head swim.

"Who are you?" she whispered, and for the first time since her mother died the world seemed just a little less frightening.

She glanced at the girl who'd entered with him. Even she seemed to realize something had changed, unclenching her fists and dropping her shoulders.

"My name is Danil," the man said. He wobbled a little and sweat beaded his forehead. "It's all right, Catherine. We're here to help."

"Help?" The tiniest spark of hope flared deep within Catherine's soul. *Help? No one can help me...can they?*

Catherine knew she was cursed. The moment her mother had died, a crippling blanket of terror had suffocated not only her world but everything around her. Threats came for her constantly, from remnant attacks to rabid animals, and once a cloud of angry bees.

She'd been on her own for two years now, thrust into a loveless marriage when her father concluded that Catherine was a bad omen; a magnet for grief and danger. He'd married her off to Coates and dusted his hands of her fate, only to meet a messy end when he ran into a remnant band on his way home from Anrock.

Catherine shuddered, remembering the bloodied and torn arm one of the traders had brought her as proof that her father had died. He hadn't run fast enough to escape the curse.

By that point Coates had decided Catherine was damaged goods. He'd attempted to lock her up, but had ended up curled into a tiny ball, weeping at the prospect of someone being confined to a small dirty windowless cell for eternity.

And that, Catherine thought wryly, was how she'd inadvertently become responsible for a city full of people; people she'd cursed with her aura of doom.

"It's not a curse," Danil told her gently.

Catherine's eyes shot open. "What are you talking about?" She knew the townsfolk had mumbled accusations, but Catherine had never confirmed their theories—even though she believed them.

"Your curse. It's just..." Danil frowned, wondering how to explain in a way she'd understand and not be frightened by. "It's magic, but it's a bit broken. It's like you're trapped in a mirror maze at a carnival."

"Magic?" Catherine asked dubiously.

"Yes, but…" Danil cocked his head to the side as if listening to something. "That's not important now. You need to stay calm and instruct your men to open the gates."

"The…gates?" Memories of her father's bloodied ring being pulled from a bitten-off finger flashed into her mind. "No. Not the gates." She shook her head and scurried back across the bed.

The surge of fear built, then fell again, subdued into a humming bubble of worry.

"Catherine, please!" Danil begged. "My people are out there and a remnant force is—"

"Remnant!" Catherine sobbed. The veneer of control crumbled and Danil staggered under the weight of her terror. "No! No, no one must open the gates! They'll come in! They'll eat our arms and tear off our legs. They'll kill us all. *They'll kill us all!*"

"Catherine—"

"No!" She lifted her head, wild eyes turned to his face. "You're trapped here now. You're doomed—doomed with the rest of us."

Gasping raggedly, she skittered away from the visitor's outstretched hand. She evaded his clumsy grasp and fled, sprinting down the narrow hall and out into the street.

Tears blurred her eyes as she ran, partly from terror and partly from the blinding glare of the morning light. She hadn't been outside in… *No, don't think about that now. Hide. I have to hide!*

She spied a pile of fruit crates discarded by an alley.

Perfect.

CHAPTER TWENTY-TWO

"Danil's down," Julianne snapped as a remnant barreled toward them. "So is Polly."

It launched toward Garrett but was thrown aside when Marcus slammed into it.

"What?" Marcus whipped his head around, alarmed. "How the hell did *that* happen?" He let off a single pulse from his rifle and the remnant's head—as well as the small red shell attached to its brain stem—went flying.

Julianne shook her head slowly. "You wouldn't believe me if I told you. How long can we hold off this force? More specifically, how long can *you* hold it off?"

"If we knew how many o' the bastards were out there I could tell ye." Garrett slapped the haft of his axe against his palm. "But I'll take a guess and say they're not yer regular run o' the mill remnants." He pointed at the body on the ground. "If one's been got by the Skrima, they all are."

"Strange they'd only send one in to attack," Julianne mused. "You think they were testing us?"

"It's as good a guess as any." Marcus squinted toward the trees, eyes picking out a flash of movement among the foliage. "How many do you think are out there?"

"Mostly likely between, oh, two and two hundred o' the pricks," Garrett answered unhelpfully.

"And normal remnant wouldn't wait, they'd just attack." Julianne nodded in agreement.

"Aye. The bastards are waitin' fer somethin'."

"They may have that luxury, but we don't." Julianne turned to Marcus. "Get a weapon in every available hand. We'll fight to the death if need be."

"What about the town?" Garrett asked.

A flicker of indecision passed over Julianne's features. "Danil's in there and he's terrified. Not of anything that will hurt him," she quickly reassured the others. "It's just a spell. But she broke through his shields and she's on the run. I could hunt her down, but..." Her eyes scanned the tree line. "At what cost? You need fighters out here. You need my staff."

Garrett sucked air through his teeth. "Ye can fight all right, lass, but we don't need weapons. We need a big-assed wall between those mind-fucked forest scum and our people."

Julianne looked at Marcus. "Majority rules."

Marcus raised his hands defensively. "Don't make this my problem! You're the damn Master. You pick!"

Julianne folded her hands on the butt end of her staff, leaning on it casually. "I'm waiting, dear."

Marcus screwed up his face, then wagged a finger back and forth between the two. Julianne saw his lips move and guessed he was counting out the beats of a rhyme.

"Miney, mo!" Marcus's finger pointed squarely at Garrett when he stopped. "Looks like your fight is *inside* today, Jules."

Julianne nodded, happy that a choice was made. She'd calculated the odds as being fairly even either way, so she wasn't perturbed that he'd chosen against her—or worried about how he'd made a choice that might determine the fate of several dozen innocent people.

"Get yer ass in there then, lass." Garrett nodded to the trees, tips now glowing in the sunlight. "I don't think they'll wait too long."

Julianne turned to go but a hand touched her elbow.

"I know you're busy," Jackson began, "but can you help me?"

"Of course," Julianne replied. "What do you need?"

"Magic." Jackson gestured at his swollen knees. "I'm not likely to see this through. Oh, don't you worry about me—I've had a long life, and for the most part it's been a good one. But if this is how I'm going to go out, I'd like to have one last chance at taking out the bastards who have killed so many of my people."

Julianne hesitated. "Jackson, I'm not a healer. I wish I was."

"I can fight, it's just the pain holding me back. I don't need you to fix anything, just…hide it a bit. Make it so I can't feel my bones grind together with every step I take. If you could just dull even a bit of pain, I can take care of the rest."

"That's incredibly dangerous," Julianne said. "If I get it wrong, you could be mortally wounded and not even realize it."

"And I might be stabbed in the gut if you don't." Jackson leaned closer to her. "Please. I won't do anything stupid, and I won't hold you responsible if I die."

Narrowing her eyes at the logic of his last statement, Julianne pulled back. She watched him for a moment, eyes boring into his soul, but Jackson didn't flinch.

"Okay, but you have to *promise* you'll be careful."

Jackson nodded eagerly as Julianne's eyes began to glow, and moments later he bounced on bent knees and grinned.

"That's the ticket!"

He ran off to join the rest of his people, his movements as fluid and graceful as a man half his age.

"I'd best go before I have a long line of people asking me to do the same for them," Julianne said. Setting her shoulders, she stopped to give Marcus a brief hug and Garrett a shoulder-squeeze. "If I don't come back in time, kill some for me."

"Aye, I'll kill a hundred o' the bastards!" Garrett chuckled as she jogged toward the town gates.

She slowed as she approached the thick walls but didn't bother to shout. Instead, she whispered a phrase and her eyes lit up.

There was no one at the gate. Momentarily confused, Julianne did another mental sweep of the area. No one. The nearest mind she could connect with was a young woman huddled under her bed.

Julianne pushed through the woman's fear to take control of her mind. *Sorry. I really hate doing this, but lives depend on it.*

Julianne blinked her borrowed eyes. Twilla crawled out of her hiding spot and dusted off her dress, wobbling a little as her host adjusted to the woman's proportions.

You're tall! Julianne thought. Indeed, the girl had the long limbs of a model.

Twilla's mental presence shrank further. Between the last jolt of terror Catherine had caused and this strange intruder in her mind, Twilla was ready to give up and pass out.

No can do, Julianne told her. *I need your mind.*

Layering calm and security over the girl's mind, Julianne showed her what lay outside—a group of people just as terrified as those inside Anrock, but with real cause to feel that way.

Now, I know this is uncomfortable, but I need your help to get inside. I need to find Catherine and stop the fear she's spreading. I have to save my friends.

Through Twilla's eyes, Julianne inspected the gates. Their design was a feat of engineering beyond Julianne's comprehension. Complicated pulleys and ropes hung from the wall and there was a giant wheel to one side. Julianne had briefly noticed the contraption when Danil had entered, and now regretted not paying more attention to how it had operated.

Though Twilla wasn't intricately familiar with it, what she did know made Julianne's heart sink.

The gates were designed to be self-closing, and to open them wide would require the strength of two brawny men.

Perhaps Catherine had them made like that for a reason, Julianne thought. The young woman was clearly terrified of what lay outside the gates and had gone to great lengths to make sure they could not be opened without the consent of those inside.

Well, no harm in trying.

Twilla approached the great wall and gripped one of the spokes. She pushed with all her might, straining as her muscles and her cheeks flushed with the effort.

The gates didn't budge.

Shit! Julianne made Twilla take a step back, examining the construction once again. She spied a length of rope, one end lying on the ground and the other fastened to a pulley near the top of the wall.

That might work, Julianne thought.

Twilla grabbed the end of the rope and tucked it into the waist of her skirt, then scaled the ladder to a platform halfway up the wall.

Once there, Twilla gathered the rope and swung one end in a loose circle, then tossed it toward the top of the wall. Her first two throws missed, but the third went neatly over. The rope slid over the wall, and Julianne gently let the girl's mind go.

Tugging on the rope to make sure it was secure, Julianne began to climb.

She scaled the wall with little effort and dropped onto the platform on the other side. Twilla had already disappeared, no doubt sneaking back to her hiding spot.

At first glance the town was quiet and empty, but it didn't take long for Julianne to connect with the minds of dozens of people who had crumbled under the flood of terror Catherine had transmitted. Her desire to flee the incoming threat had sent the townspeople of Anrock running for cover.

Julianne's skin prickled as the spell washed over her, noticeable even through her shields. Julianne shook it off and sent out a thread of her own magic, seeking a familiar mind.

Danil's shield had been completely dismantled by the force of Catherine's terror. The very thought of opening the gate had sent her into a terrified spiral that had shattered Danil's attempts to calm her and inflicted her magic on *him*.

Danil? Julianne sent.

Can't fight it, he replied, mind fading as he was wracked by fear.

Find your center, she instructed. Julianne linked with his mind and gently guided him back toward the part of his mind that he had spent years training.

A mystic's center was deep within their consciousness, like a bright flame glowing at the very bottom of an abyss. It was rare for that place to be affected by another mystic—and near impossible for that tiny spark of inner peace to be affected by someone not trained to reach through the many layers of defense around it.

Danil's mind sank into the calmness, and Julianne felt his muscles relax and his knotted mind untangle. She waited until his shields were up, sturdy and stable as his training dictated.

Bitch's oath she's strong, Danil sent to Julianne.

Either that or you've been neglecting your practice, Julianne said.

What? No! I still practice every day, I swear. I know I've been distracted, but—

I was only teasing, Julianne assured him. *Is Polly okay?*

She felt his sudden shame as he realized he'd forgotten all about the girl. She waited until he had reassured himself that Polly hadn't been physically harmed and would recover from the mental effects of the spell.

Did you see anything that would suggest where she went? Julianne asked.

Danil gave the mental equivalent of shaking his head. *She was so frantic that I don't think even* she *knew where she was headed. How are things outside?*

Safe, but not for long. We need to sort this out right now. Julianne dropped her link with Danil and took a deep, calming breath.

First she needed to get those gates open so the people of Kells could find their own safe place to hide from the impending fight outside. Julianne embraced her magic at a deeper level, sending spears of consciousness out in all directions.

Julianne sensed a man hidden in a latrine, back pressed against the wall and hands over his face, and jabbed him with a compulsion strong enough to override his terror. *You. Here. Now.* She waited until he stood and shuffled outside before moving on.

You. The second guard had sought refuge in Catherine's manor but had been turned away, so he had buried himself under a mound of old hay in the stable. The stench of moldy straw made his stomach turn, but not as violently as the thought of what lay outside the gates of Anrock.

Come here. Open the gates, now.

He stood and bits of grass scratched inside his shirt. He didn't bother to shake it out, driven too urgently by the need to follow Julianne's instruction despite his gut-clenching fear.

Julianne patiently guided both men, blocking what effects of Catherine's spell she could. In some ways their unease helped. Eager to get this task over with so they could return to the illusion of safety, they trotted through the empty streets quickly.

Once both men stood before her, Julianne's efforts increased.

"Open the gates," she instructed.

A fresh wash of fear driven by months of mental conditioning resisted her mental force.

"Open. The. Gates." Sweat beaded Julianne's forehead, and she wondered just how damn strong Catherine was.

"Bastard curse it! If you don't open the Bitch-damned gates I'll throw you out there myself," Julianne snapped.

What little color remained in the men's faces drained away. They quickly moved to the wall, one taking a hold of the two pulleys while the other stood ready at the giant wheel.

"Pull!" called the first man and tugged the ropes, leaning back against their weight.

The other man used the momentum to move the wheel—slowly at first, then faster as the heavy doors swung open.

Send them in, Julianne sent to Marcus. *Now! I don't know how long it will stay open.*

Before the gate had fully opened, people started to wander inside. The townspeople of Kells looked around warily to see if they'd be evicted, but once they spotted Julianne they moved faster.

"Come on! Hurry…everyone in!" Julianne urged them through. The opening wasn't large—bodies jostled each other as they hurried to obey.

"Remnant!" The scream from outside sent a wave of fright through everyone present.

The guard on the pulleys whimpered and let go. Julianne cursed and latched onto the other.

"Hold it!" she yelled, giving even more weight to her mental control as she forced the terrified man to strain against the now-closing gate.

People shoved and pushed to get inside. They tripped over each other, and some stopped to help those who had fallen while others urged them to hurry.

When the wheel slipped from the guard's sweaty-palmed grip the doors began to swing shut faster, but the last of the refugees slipped through the narrowing space moments before they closed with a deep thud.

In the minutes it took for Julianne to confirm everyone was

inside and no one was hurt, the two guards had already fled back to their hiding places.

"This is getting ridiculous," Julianne muttered. "I need to find that girl and shut her magic down."

The only way she would be able to find Catherine was to get into her mind, which meant letting Catherine into her own. Finding her calm center, Julianne slowly let down the outer layer of her shields.

Her heart beat faster and her lungs tightened as her need for oxygen suddenly increased. As much as Julianne hated herself for what she was about to do, she knew it was necessary.

Where are you? Julianne sent the query not in a calming or soothing manner, but with the slightest hint of a threat behind it. Catherine's muddled mind was surrounded by a thick band of static, which made it impossible for Julianne to narrow down her location. Though Julianne could sense individual pockets of fear within the town, she didn't have time to go through each individually to discover which was her target

Julianne felt ripples of terror like waves spreading from a pebble dropped in water. It wasn't perfect but gave her a possible direction.

Julianne started to run, narrowing in on Catherine's location by targeting the swell of emotion's center.

She stopped when she lost her target and sent out another call. *I'm coming for you.* She fought against the guilty ache in her chest. *I opened the gates to let them in. Now I'm coming for you.*

Terror swelled in Julianne's breast, fueled by the emotion that ricocheted through the terrified city. After fighting it down to a manageable level, Julianne used it to her advantage. She looked for a way past the row of buildings that stood between her and the strongest projection of fear. She spotted a small alley, which was obscured by a pile of old crates that had been dumped outside it.

I won't leave until you come out.

Julianne stumbled to a stop. *Too far.* She backtracked a few steps and closed her eyes, trying to narrow in on the sensation she had felt moments before.

Up. Julianne tilted her head to examine the windows that loomed above her.

The buildings surrounding her were clustered tightly together, making it hard to tell which one she wanted. Rather than waste time trying to narrow it down further, Julianne ducked through the nearest open door.

Floorboards creaked loudly at each step, making her heart jump and her stomach clench. Julianne allowed herself a small grin of victory. *She can hear me.* That meant her target was close.

Catherine's proximity and Julianne's lowered shields made it impossible to hide from the magic. Fear beat at the edges of Julianne's mind, held back only by the strength of her personality and many years of practice at mastering her emotions. As much as she ached to, Julianne wasn't quite ready to shut down her connection to the younger and very frightened mental magician.

Julianne paused, and as silence filled the room she heard another sound; one that had been obscured by her noisy progress.

Weeping. The terrified girl's frightened sobs made Julianne's heart lurch and guilt warred with the knowledge that her actions had been necessary. Julianne crept into the room next to her and quietly walked over to the ragged blankets that covered a shaking figure in the corner.

"I'm sorry for scaring you," Julianne said gently. Her shoulders dropped, and her chest relaxed as she resurrected her shields. "I'm here to help."

The blanket stilled for a moment, then another terrified sob escaped. Catherine couldn't hold her breath for more than a moment.

"Catherine, would you like to stop being afraid?"

The sobs halted again and though the blanket didn't move, a

voice spoke up from beneath them. "You're going to kill me, aren't you?"

"No. I don't kill good people."

The blanket heaved another gulping breath. "I'm not a good person," Catherine said in a shaky voice. "I'm cursed. I'm the reason the remnant are here."

"You're not cursed," Julianne insisted. "You're a mental magician like me, except I've had training. I can project my emotions and feel what others feel, but I can also stop that from happening."

A corner of the blanket dropped away and a glittering red-rimmed eye peeked out. The girl didn't speak, so Julianne continued.

"When a normal person gets scared," Julianne explained, "they only have to deal with their own fear. Oh, that fear can be crippling. It often is, because our world is a scary place and a lot of dangerous things live here."

The blanket dropped farther to reveal the second eye.

"But when *you* feel afraid," Julianne continued, "your magic projects that fear toward everyone around you. It also picks up their emotions, so you feel not just your emotions but theirs as well." Julianne held up thumb and forefinger two inches apart and bounced a fingertip from the other hand between the digits.

"Your emotions bounce from you to them and back to you." The finger kept bouncing. "It keeps going like that, stuck in a loop. Catherine, I know that you're afraid, but you're not nearly as scared as you think you are."

The blanket finally fell away and Catherine wiped her nose with her sleeve. "The man in my room...that was what he was trying to tell me?"

Julianne nodded.

"The magic... You said it's like yours. Can you stop it? Can you take it away from me for good?" Hope flared in Catherine's face, sending Julianne's heart plummeting to her boots. There would be no easy fix for this.

"I can teach you how to manage it better," Julianne said. "For now, though, I'm going to shield you. As long as my magic stays active, you won't be able to feel your emotions reflected back at you—nor will you be able to affect others."

Catherine gave a shaky nod. "Please, do it now."

She squeezed her eyes shut and braced herself.

Julianne crouched in front of the girl and took Catherine's hands in hers. "I can't just shut down another person's magic, not without hurting them. I'll need your help to do it."

Before Julianne began, she reached out to Marcus. *Is everything still okay out there?*

Depends on your definition of okay, Marcus growled.

Julianne sucked in a sharp gasp. *Marcus, your arm!* Marcus's arm flared with pain and she felt him stumble as something hit him across the back.

Just do what you need to, he sent back. *But do it fast.* Julianne prepared to pull away, but Marcus reached out before she could.

Jules… He hesitated. *Don't come outside unless you're sure we're going to win. Your duty isn't to keep me safe, it's to protect the people inside.* He swallowed. *I love you.*

Marcus' shield slammed down, leaving Julianne with the memory of the last thing he had seen. Remnant; *hordes* of remnant with eyes glowing the wrong shade of red. The town was surrounded and her friends were outnumbered…and she wasn't there to fight with them.

"*Shit!*"

Catherine's startled flinch made Julianne regret her slip of the tongue.

"It's okay," Julianne said, soothing the girl with a soft brush of magic. Slipping into the deepest part of Catherine's consciousness, she gently encased the girl's mind in a shield and felt the near-instantaneous rush of relief as her emotions calmed.

"I can't feel them!" she breathed. "They're out of my head. I can't *feel* them anymore."

Julianne smiled as a weight lifted. Though it had been a small action in the greater scheme of things, the difference she had made to one person made her heart sing.

She waited for Catherine to adjust to her newfound reality, then gently caught her attention again.

"This is the part I need help with," Julianne explained.

She deftly guided Catherine, helping her summon her magic and stifle her outpouring of emotion. Though it was effective, Julianne knew Catherine had no real understanding of how this spell worked. It would fall away as soon as Julianne let go of the reins. She silently thanked Artemis for all the grueling training he'd put her through, hoping she had the stamina to see this through.

Once Catherine's mind was safely ensconced in a protective shield that wouldn't let magic in or out, Julianne stood. She offered a hand to Catherine, who took it.

Catherine's eyes sparkled with excitement and a grin spread across her face. "I feel...incredible! All those feelings pressing in... I thought they were mine. But they're not! They never were!"

Julianne grinned back, happy to see the relief on the girl's face —and even happier that she couldn't *feel* a single drop of it.

"What do we do now?" Catherine asked. Her brow furrowed as she recognized that this would only be the first step of many.

Julianne's eyes drifted in the direction of the gates. "We run," she said softly. She turned back to Catherine and met her gaze. "But this time we're not running away."

Catherine gave a resolute nod, awed by her newfound sense of calm. "It's strange," she told Julianne as they sped through the streets. "I still feel afraid, but nothing like before. This is like playing hide and seek in the dark compared to what I had to deal with every single day."

Julianne smiled. "I'm sure you'll get used to it."

The two women stumbled to a stop at the gates, where a cluster of people milled about talking nervously. They fell silent as Julianne and Catherine appeared hand in hand.

"What's going on outside?" a voice called.

Julianne ran her eyes over the small crowd. People from Kells and Anrock mingled, shooting anxious glances toward the sounds of fighting that drifted over the solid wall.

"The remnant are here," Julianne said. "And I need you to help me fight them."

Shocked gasps and angry curses erupted.

"You can't send us out there among those monsters!"

"You told us we'd be safe here!"

"You can't expect us to go outside. We'll all be killed!"

Julianne listened to their refusals with a growing impatience. "My friends are out there," she snapped. "They'll *die* if we don't go out there and help."

"And you think *we'd* survive for more than five minutes?" The man who spoke looked at his friends for support, which he got it in the form of eager nods and grumbles. "You came here, and you brought these monsters with you. You got your people inside, but we're not giving our lives for you."

Julianne cursed. "If you want to cower behind these walls and let those bastards dictate what kind of life you live, fine. Open the gates. I'll fight them alone if that's what I need to do."

One of the guards gave an outraged shriek. "*Open the gates?* You can't be serious. If you want those gates open, you'll have to go through me. I'm not letting those monsters into this town without a fight."

"Oh, *now* you find the balls to stand up for yourself," Julianne muttered.

"Julianne!" Polly's voice rose above the din and she hurried over. Danil trailed behind her. "What's going on?" she asked, eyeing Catherine warily.

Julianne shook her head in frustration. "The remnant are

outside and Marcus is hurt." She frowned, looking at Danil. "Hang on... Why don't you already know that?"

Danil blushed. "I *may* have overstretched myself a little while I was talking to Catherine."

A new wave of fear rose, constricting Julianne's throat. She'd counted on Danil's help to get the gates open. She pushed back the urge to rub her head to ease her growing headache. Julianne knew she didn't have the strength to hold Catherine's shields while creating new spells of compulsion.

"Can't you just..." Catherine waggled her fingers. "Magic your way past him?"

Julianne shook her head. "I can't, not without unraveling the spells protecting you. And if I do *that*, we'll have a riot. With Danil out of commission, I'm stuck." Julianne caught Catherine's glance at Polly. She shook her head. "Polly's not a mental magician."

Catherine frowned, thinking the problem over. "So if you weren't keeping my magic restrained you'd be able to get past him?"

Julianne nodded absentmindedly.

Catherine stepped in front of her. "Hit me."

Julianne gave her a confused look.

Catherine repeated herself. "Hit me! Right in the face." She pressed her lips together to stop them from trembling and squeezed her eyes tightly shut, bracing for the impact.

"Why would... Oh, you mean knock you out? Julianne asked.

Catherine nodded. "It will stop my magic, right? Coates always said that the only time he didn't have to suffer my curse was when I slept."

Danil shrugged, giving Julianne an apologetic glance. "It might be our only option, Jules."

Julianne let out a growl of frustration. "Just once—just *one time*—could they make it easy for me?"

"For Julianne! For Kells!" The voice rang over the din outside, drifting over the wall to cut through the murmurs of dissent that surrounded Julianne.

Silence fell.

"Was that Jackson?" an old woman asked.

"Yeah," a man next to her said. "Didn't you see? He stayed outside to fight with the others." He shook his head in regret. "Silly old bastard."

"Jackson? You mean Jackson from Kells? The old man?"

"That's him."

Julianne closed out the conversation bubbling around her. "If I'm going to have to do this, I may as well get it over with. Are you *sure* this is what you want?" she asked Catherine.

"Do you promise you'll—"

"To hell with it!" The old woman's bark cut off Catherine's response. "That man has more balls in his little finger than you've got in a week's worth of pants."

The grandmother turned on the guardsman and jabbed her cane at him. "You might want to cower in here, but the people of Kells know where that kind of cowardice leads. We're goin' out to fight, and you're gonna open the Bitch-damned gate so we can do it."

Julianne turned to the crowd, her mouth hanging open in shock.

"You can't! You're older than my Nan!" The guard stumbled back, almost falling on his ass as the old woman advanced.

"And do you think your Nan would be proud of you now?" she demanded.

Looking around in desperation and hoping for support, the guard was disappointed when no one stepped forward to back him up.

"I've met Jackson a time or two," a man remarked. Julianne didn't recognize him from Kells, so she guessed he was local. "The old bag is right. If that old coot can take those monsters on, so can we. I'm sick of hiding under my wife's linens. I'm going out there with them." The man hefted an iron hoe and Julianne wondered where he'd found it.

The second guard Julianne had used earlier stepped forward and put his hand on his friend's shoulder. "We're outnumbered. Good thing, too. I don't think I could live with myself if old Jackson died to protect our sorry asses—and outside our own damn town, no less."

Julianne watched silently, knowing that the next few moments would decide the fate of an entire city. She held her breath as the guard's eyes darted back and forth, his mind turning over the sudden change around him.

"All right," he said quietly. "Martha?" A woman stepped forward, holding a small child in her arms. The little girl squirmed and reached for the guard.

"You do what you need to, Dan." Martha stretched up to kiss him on the cheek. "I'll take care of Matti. Just...just make sure you come back to us in one piece."

The woman's voice broke on her last words and the child started to wail. Tears running down his cheeks, the guard strode over to the giant wheel.

Julianne called, "Wait!" and turned back to Catherine, her right hook knocking the girl out before she could even cry out. "OK, go!"

"Ready?" he called

"Pull!" came the response.

Those who had armed themselves raced through the opening doors, Julianne, Danil, and Polly amongst them. Although the amateur soldiers ground to a halt when they saw the horde of remnant, the three fighters did not. Julianne plunged into the fray, a well-placed swing of her staff snapping a Skrim off the neck of a remnant. The beast spun and yanked out the wriggling tentacle from the hole in its neck, then launched itself at a nearby remnant and tackled it to the ground, scrabbled at his foe's neck to bestow the same gift Julianne had given him.

Julianne's eyes searched the battlefield. "Marcus?" she yelled.

"Julianne!" The response came not from Marcus, but from Garrett.

Julianne fought through a tight cluster of three remnant, one of them fighting off two others. Julianne took a brief moment to assess the situation, then rammed her staff into the ribs of one of the pair fighting together. It turned to her in a red-eyed rage and a second flick of her staff broke its nose.

The remnant howled and swiped at its face. Another jab of Julianne's staff aimed at the swollen blue bruise on its side made the beast stumble to its knees.

It quickly pushed to its feet, wobbling as it clutched at a protruding bone.

"I'm almost starting to feel bad for your hosts." She shrugged and added, "But not enough to go easy on you."

Julianne lunged, then planted her staff firmly on the ground and used its leverage to push herself forward. Her boot slammed into a remnant's chest and blood and organs squeezed out through the hole in its side. She landed on top of the beast and slit its throat.

"Sorry, I don't have time to do this delicately."

Julianne rolled off her victim and saw the other two remnant still battling it out. She ignored them and raced toward Garrett.

"This would be so much easier if you were a little taller," Marcus grumped.

His right arm, roughly bound with strips of shirt and dripping blood, was wrapped around Garrett's shoulders. The other balanced his rifle on his hip and tried to aim the weapon, but Garrett's jolting movements made it hard for him to even stand.

"No, it would be *easier* if ye hadn't stabbed yerself in the foot," Garrett snapped.

"I *told* you, it was a remnant with a knife!"

Garrett chuckled. "Admittin' ye let one o' the bastards get that close ta ye doesn't make ye sound any smarter. I'm sure your girl-friend will agree. Right, Julianne?"

Marcus lifted his head, heart swelling with joy to see Julianne sprinting toward them. She stumbled to a halt.

"What the hell happened to your foot?" she asked

"A remnant stabbed me," Marcus explained mournfully. "I can't put any weight on it, so Garrett here is acting as my left leg."

"Why the *hell* did you let a remnant get that close?" she snapped.

Garrett hooted with laughter. "What did I tell ye? *Left!*"

Garrett whirled to the left, Marcus wheeling around with him on one leg. Lifting the rifle, Marcus let off a round that sent a remnant flying backward to crash into another.

Garrett stopped and Marcus took the opportunity to slither to the ground. Garrett leaned on his knees, panting, and said, "Bitch of a fight we've got here."

"Doesn't look like anything we can't handle," Julianne said.

Garrett shook his head. "Ye'd think that if ye didn't know there's at least a dozen or more behind the tree line."

"A dozen?" Julianne asked, looking around warily. "Or *more?*"

"Aye. They attacked as one force, but some retreated when they couldn't get close enough to feel the sweet gift of me sword in their face."

Julianne's heart skipped a beat and she looked back. Although the villagers were holding their own to a degree, they wouldn't be able to withstand a second influx of the monsters.

As if the thought triggered their arrival, a cacophony of war cries sounded from the forest.

Garrett and Julianne cursed simultaneously.

"Well, we're fucked now." Garrett threw his axe down and flung his hands in the air in frustration. He turned to Marcus. "Ye'll have to sit here on yer ass. I've got work to do."

Before she could stop him, Garrett whisked his axe up from the ground and sprinted toward the oncoming horde. As he ran he lifted the weapon and swung it above his head, bellowing a war cry in some ancient and unintelligible rearick language.

"Do you think he'll make it out alive?" Marcus asked, bored.

Julianne's breath caught in her throat. "That depends on what that second group has in mind."

She lifted a hand and turned Marcus's attention to another group of remnant coming from the east. They must have circled around the city, and now sprinted through the clear space between the thick walls and the overgrown forest.

"Now we're *really* fucked," Marcus said.

—

"Danil!" Polly said, excitement rising. "Look!"

"You don't need to point, remember?" Danil said with a chuckle. The laughter died as he saw what was coming. "Bitch's britches. We're completely fucked!"

"Danil, if that's what I think it is, we might actually get out of this alive," Polly said.

"What do you mean?"

"Watch," Polly said, her voice barely above a whisper.

Danil darted in front of her to slice the arm of an attacking remnant. Polly hadn't even noticed the attack, too enthralled by the oncoming group of enemies.

"I know the odds seem pretty stacked against us," Danil said. "And it feels like there's no hope, and therefore no point… But I still need a little help here."

"What? No! Danil, you don't understand." Polly grabbed his arm and pulled him back to face her. She squeezed it hard, trying to get his wandering attention. "I think they're coming to *help* us!"

Danil spun to face another attacker, wondering if the situation had finally caused Polly to lose her mind. Still, he couldn't help but watch as the two remnant hordes collided.

"Oh. My. God." Danil watched in awe as the two groups

erupted into battle. A nearby Skrim-controlled remnant spun in shock, then broke off mid-fight to run toward the battle.

"What the *hell*?" Danil asked.

"I told you!" Polly dropped his arm to clap excitedly. "Danil, the remnant hate the Skrima even more than they hate us. Remember back in Kells? You didn't believe me, but I *know* that remnant changed after that Skrim infected it."

"Well paint me pink and call me Polly," Danil muttered.

"Sweetheart, this isn't the time to be discussing your fetishes. We've got a battle to win!"

Danil erupted into laughter, almost falling over with the force of it. "Come on," he wheezed once he had himself somewhat under control. "Let's go give your new friends a hand."

Danil and Polly took off running toward the battle as confused men and women watched.

"For Kells!" Jackson yelled from nearby.

Polly darted a glance over her shoulder and saw him running with them.

"For Anrock!" The guard, Dan, waved his sword in the air in solidarity and dashed toward the battle.

"For humanity!" Polly screamed, adrenaline coursing through her veins as she reached the unlikely battle.

She plunged into the messy, noisy press of bodies, slashing and stabbing and swiftly spinning to block attacks from the remnant who turned on her.

She swung high, then leaned back as Danil swung low. They slammed their backs together, slowly turning in a circle as their weapons flashed, striking and parrying as their enemies died.

Bodies fell and Skrima shattered. With the help of their mortal enemies, the people of Irth fought for their lands.

And they won.

CHAPTER TWENTY-THREE

Julianne yanked her sword back in time to avoid taking off a nearby remnant's nose.

The beast spared her a dull-eyed glance and gave a brief nod before it crushed the red shell in its hands. Blood and ichor oozed between its fingers, and without bothering to wipe the mess off the remnant flicked the crushed Skrim's body to the ground and bounded away.

As the dusty silence of a battle fought and won slowly crawled over the field, Julianne stumbled toward Marcus on tired feet. She gratefully accepted the arms he wrapped around her and sighed into his chest.

"I'm still trying to decide if I'm dreaming or if I've gone mad," Marcus commented with a sigh of his own. "Were the remnant really helping us?"

"I don't think they were helping *us* so much as destroying the Skrima. They came for a purpose, and for whatever reason, they decided to leave us alone when they were done." Julianne looked up at him through tired but happy eyes. "We were just lucky. So very, very lucky."

"Are ye lovesick fools comin' in or what?" Garrett barked at them. "Ye look like yer both about ready ta have a nap on the grass. Nothin' *wrong* with sleeping outside, mind, but this muck ain't fit fer a pig."

Julianne looked down at her boots, pulling a face at the blood, slime, and broken red shells beneath them. "I wouldn't sit in this, let alone lie down in it."

She pulled away from Marcus and took his weight on her shoulder as they walked back toward the town they had just rescued. Both raised weary hands to wave at those they passed.

Far from a trained army, the soldiers on this battlefield were battered and bruised. They bore not only the wounds of a tough fight but the twin burdens of age and frailty.

That only made Julianne's chest swell further. "Marcus, did you ever think we would find such brave people?"

"After what happened back in Arcadia? I never doubted we'd find other brave souls or *good* people, but this? This has exceeded my wildest expectations."

"Mine too," Julianne whispered as they looked around. "Look —there's an old cart over there. You can rest in that."

Marcus wrinkled his nose. "It stinks of moldy hay."

"Trust me, it's an improvement. Hold on—"

Marcus waited patiently as Julianne's eyes glowed. She nodded, then blinked as if startled. After a shake of her head, her eyes cleared.

"Who was that?" Marcus asked, quite familiar with Julianne's silent mental conversations.

"It was Bastian." She frowned and cocked her head to one side as her eyes glowed briefly again.

"Over here!" Polly called, running over with Danil.

"What is it?" Danil asked, still short of breath.

Julianne still looked slightly bewildered. "Bastian just contacted me. He wanted to check if everything was going all right." She paused.

"And?" Danil asked impatiently.

"And...Hadley's with him." Julianne fell silent again.

"Hadley?" Danil asked incredulously. "Wasn't he with Hannah? Last I heard they'd gone to where the snow never ends. Why is he back?"

Julianne lifted serious eyes to her friends, worry etched deeply into her face. "He's come to ask us for help. Ezekiel needs us. To send Hadley all this way? Something is very, very wrong."

FINIS

AUTHOR NOTES AMY HOPKINS
WRITTEN MAY 25, 2018

It feels like ages since I wrote this book! It kinda has been, at least compared to my usual schedule. Before you pull out the pitchforks, go look at that cover again. Isn't it shiny? THAT'S why I had to wait.

All six (wow, six books already?) books have beautiful new skins, and they look amazing!

Meanwhile, it's been an interesting time to be in the bowels of the KGU. My AOM compatriots are brewing something... Zeke has a new trick up his sleeve... and for a brief snip, at least, I get to work with my old pal PJ again! He's loads of fun to write with and I'm really glad we could team up for... the thing. The thing I'm not allowed to talk about. (Don't tell Chris and Lee I talked about it, ok? They might decide they have to kill me.)

All our characters have been thrown into a giant melting pot and will then branch back off into their own books for more adventures, before coming back together for one last epic showdown. My part in that will be the final Jules book. Why? Well, she's had one hell of an adventure, but now she's ready to hang up her boots and take some time off.

I'm not closing the gates on more AoM though. If there is something you'd love to see, hit me up. It may just spark an idea I can't let go of :)

Happy Reading, guys!

Amy.

AUTHOR NOTES - MICHAEL ANDERLE
WRITTEN MAY 28, 2018

First, THANK YOU for not only reading this book, but reading through our author notes here at the end.

Right now, I'm about 15,000 feet in the air on a Delta jet heading from Boston to New York Kennedy.

I'm sure I'll get higher ;-) (*No, I couldn't resist.*)

As Amy mentioned 'something' is happening in the Age of Magic. It is interesting the authors writing inside of the age are creating this...*story* together that exceeds the <redacted> of what they <redacted> and I'm having this cool moment as the Universe creator watching my collaborators take off with something and go in a direction I had not intended and it is very edifying to me.

Why?

Because it means the authors inside of the Age like *working and being* with each other. They enjoy their characters, the situations and the opportunities to engage in this little area of the Kurtherian Universe has brought them and are willing to tackle <redacted> which is not so easy to accomplish for their fans, and themselves.

The premise is <redacted> and the different characters (redacted, redacted and redacted) will <redacted> until the

<redacted> try to <more redactions…Was Michael *nucking futs* when he tried to give out these hints? Seriously, it's like he was high when he wrote this.*>

OK, I get it!

Alright, so I can't say anything about <redacted>, I get it.

Since I can't talk about *that*, let's talk about the new covers!

Last year, I started a plan to build the capabilities for 3D work into my pipeline. With Protected by the Damned covers helping to hone our skills, I spoke with Amy to see if she would like to use these 3D model capabilities and redo the covers for her series?

And she agreed! (Well, once we showed her one of the examples (or maybe it was two.))

Since then, she has been on a tear to get the covers all redone in order to release THIS book. I hope you like them (once they are all released.)

So, why did I want to start producing 3D model covers in the first place if I have amazing model shot photography? Because I'd like to provide short snippets (vignettes) of video stories with our characters. The problem is video is *REALLY* expensive to produce.

If you follow and implement how it is done at the moment.

However, I don't accept the present expensive methodologies. Nope, I want to Indie Outlaw this stuff and if it means I take more time to get my shit together (and the necessary $$$ to accomplish this) then so be it.

However, my goal is to produce good quality (not great, not perfect) stuff for about $1,000 or less for each 90 seconds. If I can manage that, I might be able to pull some cool stories together and 'amaze' the fans.

Wouldn't that be cool?

I just realized typing these author notes that maybe *YOU* (or you in Houston…Or you in Austin, Tx or you in Louisiana, Massachusetts, California, England, Germany, Australia Arizona etc. etc. etc.) reading these author notes might *ALREADY* know how to do what I hope to accomplish, or know someone(s) who do.

I'm willing to be told to go look somewhere to see cool stuff. If you know of cool stuff, drop a link on the Protected by the Damned Group (it's smaller) or in the Kurtherian Gambit group message me directly.

Either way, let's create some wonderful fun together, shall we?

Ad Aeternitatem,

Michael Anderle

*I've never actually been high in my life. However, working on some of these projects late into the night with travel fatigue and police and/or fire siren's constantly going off down in the street below does make me loopy.

CONNECT WITH THE AUTHORS

Amy Hopkins Social
Website:
https://amyhopkinsauthor.com
Facebook:
https://www.facebook.com/thespellscribe

Connect with Michael Anderle

Website: http://lmbpn.com
Email List: http://lmbpn.com/email/

Social Media:

https://www.facebook.com/LMBPNPublishing
https://twitter.com/lmbpn
https://www.instagram.com/lmbpn_publishing/
https://www.bookbub.com/authors/michael-anderle

BOOKS BY AMY HOPKINS

Books from Amy Hopkins

The Talented Series

Dream Stalker: Talented Book 1

Barrow Fiend: Talented Book 2

Truth Taker: Talented Book 3

Faery Teind: Talented Book 4

A New Dawn

With Michael Anderle

Dawn of Destiny

Dawn of Darkness (2)

Dawn of Deliverance (3)

Dawn of Days (4)

Broken Skies (5)

Broken Bones (6)

Penny and Boots

*With Michael Anderle

Snakes and Shadows

Werewolves and Wendigo

Pixels and Poltergeists

Bunyips and Billabongs

Other Books

Realm of the Nine Circles

BOOKS BY MICHAEL ANDERLE

For a complete list of books by Michael Anderle, please visit

www.lmbpn.com/ma-books/

All LMBPN Audiobooks are Available at Audible.com and iTunes. For a complete list of audiobooks visit:

www.lmbpn.com/audible